HATING
JESSE HARMON

WITHDRAWN

ROBIN MIMNA

IMMORTAL WORKS
Salt Lake City

Immortal Works LLC
1505 Glenrose Drive
Salt Lake City, Utah 84104
Tel: (385) 202-0116

© 2022 Robin Mimna
https://www.robinmimna.com

Cover Art by Rebecca Barney
barneydesign.com

All rights reserved, including the right to reproduce this book or portions thereof in any form whatsoever. For more information visit https://www.immortalworks.press/contact.

This book is a work of fiction. Names, characters, businesses, organizations, places, events and incidents either are the product of the author's imagination or are used fictitiously. Any resemblance to actual persons, living or dead, events, or locales is entirely coincidental.

ISBN 978-1-953491-40-4 (Paperback)
ASIN B0B7G4ZXBG (Kindle)

For my beautiful sisters Amy & Heather, because caterpillars need to stick together.

To Robert & Veronica Hart, Debbie Kunz, George Meier, Laura Andrews, and all the members of the FWA's Daytona Area Fiction Writers. Without your expertise and support, this book would still be a dream.

Prom Night

Frances

"Our new prom queen is..." Kevin paused as he slipped the gold-rimmed card from its envelope. Beads of sweat prickled my forehead. Beside me on stage, Lena's red sequined dress almost blinded me under the roasting stage lights. For the first time since I've known her, she looked nervous.

Nick, already crowned king, stood off to the side and waited along with everyone else, but all I could think about was my throbbing right hand. My battered knuckles threatened to start bleeding. I grimaced and hid my hand behind my back. Seriously, if anyone expected answers, they could ask the other guy.

Kevin cast me a bright, practiced smile, and I squeezed my eyes shut against a roll of nausea.

"Frances Hughes!" Kevin yelled, and the room erupted in applause. Before I could absorb what it all meant, Kevin placed a tacky glitter crown on my head.

Lena's shoulders slumped, and I *almost* felt bad for her as she shrank from the traditional congratulatory hug and stalked off stage.

Kevin shoved the microphone in my face. I recoiled as if he'd tried to hand me a live snake. He shook it at me again and silently mouthed, "Say something."

I took the microphone with my good hand and peered into the crowd. Naomi was right up front, her reassuring smile a beacon in the dark. The noise of the crowd died down in anticipation of whatever heartwarming platitudes I might offer as their newest prom queen, but I didn't have the heart to tell them that so far, the whole thing had sounded better on paper.

I was probably the most absurd prom queen of all time: a cynical, *dateless* bookworm who was sweating through her plus-size dress and sporting the busted knuckles of a prizefighter. So, how had it come to this? I looked into the crowd, contemplating all the twists and turns that set me upon the crooked throne of my high school social empire, and just knew that somehow this whole thing *had* to be Jesse Harmon's fault.

CHAPTER 1

Jesse

One month earlier

There was nothing worse than running laps. My legs and chest tightened as I pushed my aching limbs across the football field. I'd almost finished my final circuit, the Florida humidity pulling air from my lungs as Chris cruised by, not even breaking a sweat. I thought about sticking my leg out to trip him, but I barely had enough energy to catch up, let alone make him fall. No matter how hard I strained, I fell farther and farther behind. Best friend or not, it looked like breaking his legs was the only way to beat him.

A sharp whistle prevented me from putting my succeed-by-assault-and-battery plan into action. Coach Hughes corralled us into a circle and grunted as he took a knee. He'd been an athlete once, but now he limped when he stood too long. There was nothing wrong with his lungs, though. He blew the whistle again, and my eardrum nearly exploded.

"All right, pay attention. We have our first spring scrimmage coming up, and I want everyone at practice because we will be focusing on drills." This gruff declaration provoked a series of groans around the circle until they were silenced by one of Coach's sharp looks. "Just because regular season is over, it's no excuse to slack off. Understood?"

What did he think we were doing? There was so much sweat

pouring down my face it felt like sixty gallons of Gatorade wouldn't be able to replace the water I'd lost.

Coach was a decent enough guy, but I'd like to see him run a few drills.

"Harmon, are you listening?"

"Yeah, Coach." I replied, praying he wouldn't make me run extra laps. I was running out of body fluids.

"Harmon, my office. The rest of you finish drills and clean up."

I looked at Chris, who shrugged and headed back to the field. Reluctantly, I followed Coach into the gym. The squeaking shoes of the girls' volleyball team echoed off the high ceilings.

Coach's office was attached to the locker room and smelled how you'd expect a coach's office to smell: a mix of old socks and that aerosol spray people use on bowling shoes. A small frame stood on his desk, but the picture was turned away from me. A large glitter-smeared poster on the back wall read "West Pine High School Chargers" in the school's blue and gold colors. The rest of the walls were covered with college football posters.

We both sat down. Coach slipped on a pair of reading glasses and punched a few keys on a computer that looked older than I was. "Miss Blackwell tells me you're failing English."

Uh-oh.

"You know the deal. If you can't keep your grades up, you can't play. So, what do you plan to do about it?"

We stared at each other. I knew he wanted a response, but all I could call up was a half shrug.

"Blackwell says she'll give you a chance to turn in a paper you were supposed to submit last week. Something about Shakespeare?"

I nodded. It sounded familiar. Then again, there were a few assignments I hadn't bothered to tackle.

He eyed me over the brim of his glasses. "As a favor to me, she's giving you till the end of the month to finish. Don't come back on the field until it's done. My daughter, Frances, has agreed to meet you in the library tomorrow after school and help you." He muttered that last part.

"What?"

"If you're still looking to make varsity next year, then your butt better be in that library after school tomorrow," he said sternly. "Questions?"

I shrugged again. It didn't seem like I had a choice.

"Good. Now go shower," he said, waving a dismissive hand at me. I stood, but before I reached the door, he added, "You know, Frances is..." he trailed off, as if he'd thought better about what he'd planned to say. His mouth twitched, resulting in more of a grimace than a smile. "Just be patient with her."

"You can't come to practice at all? That doesn't sound so bad." Chris sat behind me on the locker room bench, the air still misty from the shower.

I ran a hand through my wet hair and slammed my locker shut. "Or games," I muttered.

"Maybe we'll actually win one, then."

I took a half-hearted swing at him, but his thin frame dodged the blow without much effort. He was kidding, anyway. We'd had an amazing season, and there was no doubt I'd make varsity quarterback next year.

"So, you actually *have* to write this paper? Like, no way out of it?"

"Don't think so. He sounded pretty serious."

"Why didn't you have Lucy write it?" Chris asked as he put on his socks.

Chris's little sister, Lucy, was a genius. At twelve, she already took high school courses part-time online. Fortunately for us, she hadn't developed a powerful sense of moral principle yet and didn't mind doing homework for cash.

"I forgot about it," I said. "And I didn't think Blackwell would make such a big deal about it. Now Coach has his daughter helping me, so he'll know if I don't show up."

Chris gaped at me. "You don't mean Frances?"

I raised an eyebrow at his horrified expression. "I guess so."

He whistled. "Man. You're toast."

"Her dad said something weird, too. What's wrong with her, anyway?" I tried to imagine what could be so scary about a girl that the mention of her name could summon so much doomsaying. "Does she have three eyeballs or something?"

"I had a class with her last year. One morning I opened the door too fast and accidentally hit her in the face."

"Ouch, nice." My initial reaction was to laugh, but Chris's frown told me he didn't find it so funny.

"I felt bad and tried to apologize, but she screamed at me and spent the rest of the semester calling me an idiot. It got old after a while."

"Well, to be fair, you are an idiot," I said, trying to sound serious but failing.

"Just don't get on her bad side. She knows how to hold a grudge."

"Whatever," I said, hoping it sounded relaxed. I didn't want Chris to think some crazy girl had the power to shake me up. "I can handle Coach and anything his daughter wants to throw at me."

CHAPTER 2

Frances

There was no one worse than Jesse Harmon. I glanced at the library clock. Of course he was late. I supposed I should've felt privileged to be spending an afternoon with one of the school's social demigods, but all I could muster was a hard knot of resentment in my stomach.

The girl running the library desk stared into space, one palm propping her mushed cheek. Her vacant expression was a perfect reflection of our collective boredom.

Silence was broken when the library doors swung open, and in strolled Jesse. He had perfect cheek bones, and his tussled golden hair shone in the overhead lights, and I couldn't take my eyes off him. I was equal parts awed by his good looks and irritated I wasn't entirely immune to them.

When he spotted me, his confident strides veered in my direction. "Frances, right?" he asked, already sounding uninterested.

The magic spell broke, and the desire to punch him made my palms itch. Not even a stupid excuse for being late? "Please don't call me Frances," I said. "Everyone calls me Franny."

"I like Frances better," he argued, the corner of his mouth twitching upward.

"Who asked you?" I shot right back at him. Did he honestly think everyone was dying to know his opinion? Or was he messing with me?

"Chill." He turned a chair around and plopped himself down. "So, how do we do this?"

This is for Dad. This is for Dad. I repeated this mantra in my head as I took a calming breath and slid the library's copy of Shakespeare's *Taming of the Shrew* across the table to him.

His brows knitted together, forming a small knot in the center of his forehead. "What's that?"

"That," I said, my words weighed down with sarcasm, "is a book."

He rolled his eyes. "Yeah, but how did you know what story I was supposed to do?"

He was even more clueless than I'd imagined. "Blackwell emailed my dad. The assignment was to write a report on any Shakespeare play. I chose *The Taming of the Shrew*."

He frowned. "How come you get to pick?"

"Because I'm the one who's helping you," I shot back, louder than I meant to. The girl at the front desk glanced over at us, and I lowered my voice. Was he going to argue about every detail? "Just read it this weekend, and we can start writing your paper next week."

He hesitated to pick up the book, as if he were afraid he'd catch some horrible social disease from its musty pages. After a second's consideration, he slid the book back over to me. He leaned closer and flashed me a smile I'm sure more than one silly girl had seen and worshipped before. "I'll bet you've read it, right? Can't you just tell me what happens?"

Where is a blunt object when a girl needs one? Perhaps smashing his head in would get the point across. "Read the play," I said, "and then I'll help you. Believe it or not, I have better things to do than help you skim through English to whatever beer-guzzling college frat house the future has in store for you." I pushed the book back over to him and stood up before he could argue. On my way out, I caught the eye of the girl behind the desk, and we shared a smug look. I didn't know her, but I was still glad she approved.

"Hey, wait up," Jesse called behind me. He caught up just as I opened the door, which I purposely let shut in his face.

"Hey," he yelled, pulling the door open. "What's your problem?"

I spun around and nearly laughed at his outraged expression. This was probably the first time a girl hadn't fallen for his stupid flirting act, and now he was mad about it. "I don't have a problem," I threw at him. "You have a problem because you're the one failing English. I told you what to do. If you don't like it, you can find a more interesting place to stick that book." A small, triumphant smile touched my lips as I walked away, leaving him to contemplate the numerous prospects of my suggestion.

I SHOULD'VE KNOWN ESCAPING to my room undetected was too much to hope for. The second my foot hit the third step on the staircase, Dad bellowed my name. I swung around the stair railing and poked my head into the den. The grunts and whistles of a football game played in the background. "Yeah, Dad?"

He shot me a side glance, unable to peel one eye off the TV. "How'd the tutoring go?"

"Fine."

"Just fine, Kitten? Do you have anything to add?"

The question stumped me. Did I actually have to tell him how badly things went with Jesse? Dad would probably blame me. "I'll get back to you on that," I said. "Where's Mom?"

"At a meeting," he said, already reabsorbed into the game.

"Oh," I muttered and trudged upstairs.

Mom, the alcoholic. The alcoholic who loved telling people she was an alcoholic. After bouncing in and out of several rehabs, the woman I'd known vanished. That's when she started going to AA meetings and accepted the alcoholic "higher power" into her life. Sober almost a year, any time things didn't go her way, she hopped in the car and went straight to the nearest meeting. Her entire world was about recovery. Working on her recovery, talking to her sponsor about her recovery, giving inspirational talks about her recovery "journey." She was the Mother Theresa of alcoholics. Meanwhile, I hadn't said a word to her in five days, and she still hadn't noticed.

Upstairs, I checked my email and browsed a few random TikTok videos. I had to click my way through weight loss ads and plus-size clothing offers. Was my laptop trying to tell me something? I wasn't a circus freak, but I wouldn't be caught wearing Spandex anytime soon. I wasn't exactly what Jane Austen might describe as a "reputed beauty," not when I barely cleared five feet and had limp brown hair.

Finding nothing interesting online, I picked up my beaten copy of *Mansfield Park* and fell on the bed. I'd only managed to read one sentence when my cell rang. I rolled my eyes when I saw who it was but answered anyway. "Speak."

"So?" asked Naomi.

I sighed. Of course I knew what she meant, but I was determined not to encourage her. "So, what?"

"So, what happened with gorgeous football star Jesse-Freaking-Harmon, you sly girl? Spill it."

My eyes glided to the top of my head again. Apparently, there was no escape from Jesse Harmon today. "Nothing. He's an idiot. I told him to read the play, and I left."

"That's it?" she huffed, making zero effort to hide her disappointment.

"What did you think was going to happen? Dad told me to help him with his English paper, not have his baby. Besides," I said, picking at one of my fingernails, "Jesse Harmon would never associate with peasants like us under normal circumstances."

"Ugh," she moaned. "Why can't I have an interesting best friend?"

"Thanks a bunch. Are we finished? Because I was reading."

"Oh, don't be that way. You know I'm joking." A weighted pause stretched between us. "But didn't *anything* at all interesting happen?"

I frowned. Maybe I was boring. "He called me Frances."

"Ouch, bad move."

"Yes, it was."

"Oh, come on, Franny, he didn't know." Her voice betrayed a bit of a whine. "Maybe he thinks your name is sexy."

"Because that makes sense," I countered. "Are we done now?"

"Gosh, you're in a mood. You really want to go?"

Guilt washed over me. I shouldn't be short with her, even though Naomi's enthusiasm could be annoying even at the best of times. "Sorry, it's been a long day, and I'm tired. Can we talk tomorrow?"

"Sure, no problem," she said, "but are you absolutely, *positively* sure nothing interesting happened?"

I wanted to crack a joke about how bankrupt her life must be if all she had to look forward to was hearing all the insignificant details of my day, but I decided to stick with the boring truth. "Naomi, nothing happened, and nothing is ever going to happen. Guys like Jesse aren't into girls like me, and that's *fine* with me."

CHAPTER 3

Jesse

The cafeteria hummed with a hundred conversations, but it was still impossible to ignore Mike and Travis as they debated their chances of winning next week's game without me. Apparently, the coach's daughter wasn't the only one who doubted I could write a passable paper. "It's just a scrimmage, anyway," I muttered. Although I was still mad about not playing.

Chris worked his signature gag of shoving food up his nose, then asking people if he had anything on his face. José, our team's fullback, and his girlfriend were too busy making out to join the conversation.

Sarah hung from my arm like a life preserver as she rehashed the plot of some chick flick I had no interest in seeing. My phone vibrated, but when I saw my dad's number, I sent the call straight to voicemail. Sarah didn't bother to ask and kept on with her movie review, complete with ending reveal. At least I wouldn't have to see it. I tuned her out as I chased pasta salad across my plate with a plastic fork.

The sound of the cafeteria doors opening drew my attention in time to see Frances make her way through the lunch line. She wore a pair of plain, faded jeans and one of those free t-shirts you get when you give blood. Her brown hair fell over her face, as if she were deliberately hiding it. She picked up her food and walked to a table on the opposite side of the cafeteria. She sat with a girl I recognized, maybe from a class, but I wasn't sure.

Sarah hadn't caught on I wasn't listening, so I nodded a couple of times to help maintain my end of the conversation.

Suddenly, a crash stunned not only Sarah but the whole room into silence. Nick Temple howled with laughter at a girl whose lunch painted the floor. She was short and wore mismatched clothes: a striped shirt and purple pants. Her orange high-top sneakers were bright enough to direct traffic with, and a pair of gigantic headphones with light-up cat ears rested on the top of her head. The girl slipped the headphones off her ears and stared at the floor.

Nick's friends joined in, which encouraged him to keep going. Nick had been on the football team with us until it was obvious that he wouldn't make varsity and he switched to basketball. He was the type of guy you know will peak in high school. Still laughing, he asked the girl if she was nuts when she started tapping her head with her palm like a broken clock, ticking the same terrible second over and over.

"Are you even listening to me?" Sarah asked, turning my chin with her hand and forcing me to look at her.

"Yeah."

She smirked. "Okay. So, what was I talking about then?"

"Uh, prom?"

She beamed. It was an easy guess because lately prom was the only subject that interested her. "I was thinking we could get a limo," she suggested.

Her best friend, Janice, made a high-pitched noise that could have cracked fiberglass.

"Limo. Yeah, whatever," I muttered, but the conversation turned to muted background noise again as I watched Frances get up from the table, which wouldn't have been interesting if her friend hadn't shot out a hand as if trying to stop her.

For a second, I figured she'd gone to refill her drink, but instead, she slipped by the girl on the floor who was still drumming her head with a steady rhythm. She walked over to Nick, and in a single fluid movement, Frances casually let her drink slip from her hand, and its contents dumped all over Nick's head. "Oops," she said, loud enough for everyone to hear. "My fault."

Nick shrieked and flew out of his seat like he'd received an electric shock. His scream was high and loud, and the entire room erupted in laughter. Judging by his shrill pitch, that drink hit sub-zero temperatures.

The spectacle seemed to snap the drummer girl out of her stupor, and with everyone's attention focused on Nick, she bolted to the nearest exit, leaving Frances and Nick to glare at each other over a puddle of icy soda.

Laughter gave way to loaded silence as everyone waited to see what would happen next.

"What's your problem, you crazy bitch?" snarled Nick as he held his soaked shirt away from his chest.

A chorus of "Oohs" issued from surrounding tables, but Frances shrugged it off, not taking the bait. She looked at him as if he were a wad of gum beneath her shoe, turned her back on him, and walked out of the cafeteria.

Nick, looking astonished by the turn of events, snatched a handful of napkins and stormed off in the opposite direction.

After they were gone, conversations resumed, and everyone slowly moved on.

"Oh my gosh, she ruins everything," Sarah said as she pulled her long blonde hair into a ponytail.

"Who?" I asked, surprised by her reaction.

She pointed to the puddle of soda on the floor where Nick used to be. "Frances. She's completely nuts."

"I know, right?" squawked Janice, like a parrot repeating a practiced phrase. "My sister's friend lives down the street from her and told me the cops are always at her house. I'll bet she's got Multiple Personality Disorder or something."

"Crazy, maybe. But that *was* pretty funny," added Chris.

My gaze lingered on the door where Frances had exited as the bell rang. Sarah tugged on my jacket, kissing me lightly on the lips. "You okay?"

Picking up my tray, I forced a smile. "Yeah, sure."

MOM WAS on the phone when I got home. She waved from the kitchen and turned away, but not before I caught a glimpse of her tense expression. I didn't have to ask who she was talking to. I went straight to my room, pulled the copy of *The Taming of the Shrew* from my bag, and flopped onto the bed. Everything Shakespeare wrote sounded like an alien language. How did anybody read this?

"Fear not, my lord," I read aloud. "We can contain ourselves, were he the veriest antic in the world." I wondered if Frances would know if I read the book or looked it up on Wikipedia. There was a knock at my bedroom door, and I let the book fall on my chest. "Yeah?"

Mom came in and sat on the bed. She absently plucked the book from my chest and examined the cover. "Your father says he tried to call you earlier." She paused and tried to catch my eye, but I refused to look at her. "He says he misses you."

"Whatever," I said, staring straight at the ceiling. There was a small water stain forming just above my headboard I'd never noticed before. "He shouldn't be calling me while I'm at school anyway."

She sighed and rubbed her temple. Worry lines creased her forehead and the area underneath her eyes had grown darker. She wasn't sleeping again. "You have to talk to him at some point."

My hands tensed into fists at my sides. "Why do you keep defending him?"

"I'm not defending his *behavior*, but I don't want my son to grow up without his father."

"Well, we don't always get what we want, do we?" I snapped, but my surge of anger fizzled into regret when I saw the hurt on her face. If anyone had gotten the short end of the stick, it was Mom.

I shot up and hugged her. "I'm sorry. I didn't mean it."

She hugged me back. "It's okay," she said, but I could already see the moisture collecting in her eyes and cursed inwardly. "This isn't easy for either of us. But someday you will want your dad around."

I wanted to tell her she was wrong. After what he did, I wasn't sure I ever wanted to see him again.

She nodded and stood up. "I'm glad to see you reading."

Shakespeare's stupid face scowled at me from the cover, and I couldn't help but think he looked overly confident about his talent. "It's for school."

She touched the top of my head before leaving, and I stared at the closed door for a few minutes until I was sure she was back in her room. As a diversion, my mind turned to the scene in the cafeteria. Frances was a pain in the ass, but I hadn't expected those powers could be used for good.

Like a moth drawn to a bug zapper, my thoughts returned to Dad. *He could have helped me with this stupid paper if he hadn't left.* Again, I tried to push the thought away, but the idea that the family we'd had was gone forever wouldn't fade.

CHAPTER 4

Frances

"I've decided Webb Harris is taking me to prom," announced Naomi with a flourish as she threw herself up against her locker in a mock swoon. She wore a vintage green poodle skirt and frilly black top. Her dark hair was tied back with an ivory ribbon. Her favorite combat boots were practically worn down to the soles.

"Oh yeah?" I replied, suppressing an eye roll. "Does *he* know that?"

"Not yet, but he's shy. I can't just spring it on him." She nodded toward the glass double doors that opened into the courtyard. Outside, Webb sat on a bench, curled into a ball like a shy cat, his nose in a book.

Webb was a quiet guy with reddish curly hair that covered his eyes, which were usually cast down at what he was reading. Although Naomi tended to like dark, aloof guys, I struggled to picture my extroverted friend with such a shy and moody loner. But Naomi was nothing if not persistent. If she wanted to go out with him, I doubted he would have much say in the matter.

"Okay," I said, "So, when are you going to ask him?"

"Ask who, what?" interrupted Trevor as he slipped between us to get to his locker. As outrageous as Naomi dressed, Trevor cultivated a more conservative look. He wore pressed khakis and a stylish button-down shirt that praised his brown skin. This look cultivated his professional approach to all social situations and gave him an air of authority on the latest gossip.

"Webb Harris is taking Naomi to prom, but nobody's told him."

"Right," he said as he worked the combination on his locker. "Are you sure he wouldn't be more interested in going with me?"

Naomi stared at Trevor without blinking. Obviously, she hadn't considered that possibility. "You don't think he's gay, do you?"

"I'm messing with you," said Trevor, but winked at me. "He's too boring to be gay." Trevor had come out to his friends and family on the last day of middle school, because he'd said he wanted to start high school as his most authentic self.

Naomi stuck her tongue out at him. "Well, I think he's great."

"But you still haven't told us how you're going to get him to take you to prom," I pointed out. "He's not exactly a party person."

"Well," she said, practically pushing Trevor out of the way to get to me, "he's way too shy to agree to go with me," she explained. "So, I'm going to have to trick him."

"Because that's way easier than asking him." I poked my finger at her forehead, but she swatted it away. "Whatever weirdo plan you have in your head, it's not going to work." But I knew it was pointless to warn her. Naomi had a history of pursuing terrible ideas to their inevitably disastrous end.

"You let me worry about that. Guys are inherently dumb. Tricking him won't be as hard as you think."

"Uh, excuse me," chimed in Trevor, raising his hand. "Guy. Standing right here. Who can hear perfectly."

We ignored him, and Trevor muttered something about women under his breath that didn't sound very flattering.

While Naomi regaled us with her thoughts on the color of Webb's eyes, Trevor leaned closer and whispered into my ear. "Ever feel like you're being watched?" His eyes drifted toward the hallway intersection where a pair of wide eyes, crowned with unmistakable cat-eared headphones, stared at us, half hidden behind a concrete wall.

Her name was Sonny. I knew that because when she transferred in the middle of the school year, the principle decided that Dad and all the rest of the teachers should complete training on teaching kids with autism. Sonny seemed to avoid people at all costs. I wasn't sure anyone had actually heard her talk.

"Maybe she wants to say thank you for putting Nick in his place," Trevor suggested.

It was a reasonable theory, although, if I were honest, I hadn't done it for Sonny. Any excuse to give Nick's flaming ego a much-needed cool down was always welcome.

Uncomfortable with her gawking, I waved, but she only slunk further behind the wall and continued to stare at me like I was the next sideshow act at the circus.

Frustrated, I turned my attention back to Naomi's babbling until Trevor said, "Hey, look who it is," and gestured down the hallway.

Jesse Harmon strolled by, one arm draped over his girlfriend's shoulders. I frowned and looked away from her perfect body. Being effortlessly skinny should be regulated and taxed, then paid in stipends to plus-size girls so we could afford better clothes.

"Hello? Earth to Franny," said Trevor.

"Sorry, what?"

"Aren't you helping that gorgeous quarterback with his English paper?"

I shushed Trevor and crammed a book in my locker, careful to keep my back turned until Jesse and his girlfriend were out of sight. "Your point?"

"Well, let's see," he said, threading his fingers together. "You get to spend an hour or two alone with one of the hottest guys in school. Uh, hello? I don't need a point."

"We're just studying, Trevor," I said, my voice sounding sullen.

"Are you studying?" He nudged me, "or are you," he winked, "*studying?*"

I narrowed my eyes. Trevor loved to make me blush, but I wasn't in the mood for his immature brand of humor. "Drop it, okay?" I said through clenched teeth.

Trevor bristled. "Jeez, sorry. I was only asking. Anyway, Naomi, why were we even talking about prom? Didn't we agree we were too mature for it?"

I avoided Naomi's concerned look. "Right, prom is for losers," I muttered.

Thankfully, the bell rang, ending our conversation. The hallway emptied, and I again felt unfamiliar eyes on the back of my neck, but when I turned to look, Sonny was gone.

WALKING out of the school's main entrance, someone tried to snatch my backpack off my shoulders. As a reflex, I spun around, nearly ripping the person's hand off in the process.

"Hey!" yelled Jesse, pulling his hand away. "I got strap burn from your backpack."

His tone was accusatory, and I gaped at him, far too irritated to be concerned about his injury. "Well, maybe you shouldn't have tried to mug me," I snapped.

He shook his hand to relieve some of the pain. "I wasn't," he started, but stopped and just stared at me. His look was intense and appraising in a way that made me want to glance away, although I didn't.

"I mean, I didn't mean to," he said. "I was just trying to get your attention."

"Okay," I said, shifting my weight around. "You have it. What do you want?"

"I, uh, wanted to..." He stumbled over his words, which surprised me. What the hell was he nervous about?

"I wanted to say sorry for being a jerk the other day, but I really need to finish that paper."

He was apologizing? For a second, I briefly considered returning the gesture for trying to slam the library door in his face, but I silently squashed the idea. There was no need to surrender the high ground.

He appeared more agitated the longer I stood gaping at him. Finally, he turned to go, but I held my arm out to stop him. My mouth felt dry and thick. "See you tomorrow after school to go over what you've read?"

The tightness in his jaw relaxed a little. "That'd be great."

"Okay," I said, caution clouding my words. "See you then." Securing my backpack around my shoulders, I silently cursed when I glanced back and he caught me looking.

MOM'S CAR wasn't in the driveway, so I dropped my stuff at the door and flipped on the kitchen light. She hadn't bothered to make dinner. In this respect, things weren't much different from when she was drinking.

I took out a package of chicken and a box of rice. While I waited for the oven to preheat, my phone chirped with a text message. Dad had been working to embrace technology. A year ago, a text message from him would have been unheard of.

Bill said there was a problem at lunch yesterday. Bill was Dad's best friend and our school janitor, but it also appeared he'd taken a second job as a spy.

Just an accident. No big deal. I replied.

I imagined Dad texting between plays and smiled. My phone chimed in response: *Behave yourself. Love you.*

I deposited the phone back in my pocket, not bothering to try and explain. This wasn't the first time Nick Temple and I had clashed. Before high school divided our small assembly into larger schools of fish, Nick and I had been friends. But somewhere between the days of kickball and my first brooding crush on David Huff in the seventh grade, everything changed. The good-looking, athletic kids gravitated to sports and cheerleading, while gossips and broods turned toward the student newspaper or drama. Computer coders, well, they became older coders, and that left Trevor, Naomi, and me: a gay kid, a hopeless optimist, and a fat girl all exposed to the ravages of high school censure.

Maybe if I had taken my hits like everyone else, things might have been different. But over the years, I learned that Nick's biggest weakness was his pride, and I took every opportunity to damage it. That's how it started. Nick would make fun of me, and I would do something horrible in return. Over the years, the rivalry only grew more brutal.

The sound of the oven timer interrupted my quiet reflection. I noticed one of Dad's notebooks on the counter and slid it closer.

Refusing to admit what I was looking for, I flipped through the pages until I came to next year's roster and scanned the list for Jesse's name. But it had been crossed out with a note scribbled into the margin that said *replace*. Before he'd been cut, Jesse had been written into the varsity quarterback position.

I slammed the notebook shut and pushed it away. Jesse was arrogant, lazy, and an all-too-willing beneficiary of the high school hierarchy that I loathed. But unlike Nick, he had technically never done anything to *me*, and the memory of his unexpected apology softened my resolve to hate him, at least a little.

"Well, Dad," I said with a spark of determination, "you said he needed a Shakespeare paper, so that's what he'll get," and ran upstairs to grab my laptop.

CHAPTER 5

Frances

I hadn't counted on how difficult it would be to get Jesse alone. All day I combed for an opening, but he was always surrounded by either his girlfriend or a gazillion random people. It also didn't help that as I tailed Jesse, I too was being followed. Plagued with the feeling of being spied on, every time I glanced behind me, a pair of pink cat-eared headphones seemed to disappear in a flash. I wasn't happy about it, but I had business to take care of, so dealing with my little stalker would just have to wait.

It wasn't until after lunch that I found Jesse chatting with only one person, and I figured that was as close to alone as I was going to get. I took a deep breath and walked up behind him, tapping him on the shoulder.

Jesse turned, and a phantom of a smile touched his lips before he assumed his usual bored expression. "Hey."

"Can we talk a minute?"

He glanced over at his friend. "You know Chris, right?"

"You look familiar," I said as I appraised his tall friend.

"Yeah," he said with too much enthusiasm. "I hit you in the face with a door once, remember?"

"Right," I said, the memory coming into focus. "How could I forget such a magical moment?"

An awkward silence grew, and I questioned if my policy of always greeting people with ruthless sarcasm was appropriate, but I quickly dismissed the idea. That couldn't be right.

We all stood in silence as Chris failed to register his cue to leave. Finally, Jesse said, "I'll see you *later*, Chris."

"Oh, yeah sure," Chris replied and headed down the hallway, but not before looking back at us a couple of times.

Jesse rolled his eyes. "So, what's up?"

My heart rate shot up, and I forgot what I was about to say. After a few unbearable seconds, reason restored, and I pulled a packet of papers from my bag and shoved them in his face. "Here," I said, a little too loudly.

He took the papers and flipped through them. "This is a paper on the *Taming of the Shrew*." He turned his gaze back to me. "I don't get it."

I shrugged as if he needed no explanation. "You're welcome."

He looked down at the papers again and pressed his lips into a thin line, which confused me, since I'd been expecting gratitude. What was the matter with him?

I didn't have to wait long to find out. The depth of his appreciation was effectively communicated when he rolled the papers up tightly and shoved them back in my face. "No thanks, Frances." Without waiting for a response he turned his back on me and walked away.

His voice held a twinge of hurt I couldn't quite believe was real. Besides, I was too irritated at his use of my name to unpack his feelings.

"Hey, wait," I said, rushing to catch him. "What's your problem? I spent all night writing that stupid paper for you."

Jesse stopped but stared straight ahead. Clearly, he was frustrated, but I had no idea why. This was what he wanted, wasn't it?

"You must think I'm really dumb," he said.

"What are you talking about?"

"If you didn't want to help, you could have said so."

I blinked at him, unsure if I'd heard him correctly. "In case you haven't noticed," I hissed, "you're about to be cut from the football team."

"Why? Because I'm not smart enough to read some stupid play?" His voice was getting louder. He was offended. Unfortunately for both of us, this revelation only fueled my outrage.

"You needed a paper, and now you have one. I helped you, Harmon. Or has your head been bashed in too many times to see that?"

He turned and glared at me, blowing long breaths out of his nostrils. His face was so colored with anger that even the tips of his ears turned a deep shade of red. "I don't need that kind of help, *Frances.*"

What happened next was involuntary. My hands balled into fists, twitching with the need to slug him. Instead, I leaned forward, nearly nose to nose with Mr. Fantastic-Football-Star, and yelled, "Stop calling me *FRANCES!*"

My voice was so loud that it echoed off the walls, and we were both stunned into silence. I glanced around as a few straggling people paused to stare at us.

A teacher poked his head out of a nearby classroom. "Everything okay out here?"

Embarrassed, I looked away and inwardly cursed my boiling temper. "Everything's fine."

Frowning, the teacher looked at Jesse who scowled in return. "Keep it down out here; people are trying to learn," he said sternly and shut the classroom door.

Neither of us said anything for an uncomfortable moment. Had I really insulted him so much? I thought about the line drawn through Jesse's name on the roster and cringed. Had I done exactly what my dad had and just assumed Jesse would fail? The idea that *I* was the one in the wrong stung me with white-hot humiliation, and color flooded my cheeks.

Looking at anything but Jesse, I was unsurprised to spot Sonny crouched by a drinking fountain about halfway down the hall. I could just make out her purple pants and orange t-shirt half hidden behind the gray metal drinking fountain. How could someone who dresses like that manage to hide so well? Realizing she'd been made, Sonny silently raised a single hand in the air, forming a thumbs up. I had no idea what she was trying to tell me, but it gave me courage to break the silence.

"Look," I said, softening my tone. "I'm sorry, okay? I saw my dad was going to cut you from next year's varsity roster, and I didn't want that to happen."

He looked at me, his expression unreadable. "Why do you care?"

The question caught me off guard. "Care is a strong word."

He rolled his eyes and fixed his gaze over my head. I bit my lip against tossing another insult in his direction. "Look, if you don't want the paper, okay. But," I struggled to push words through clenched teeth, "I can still help you if you want."

His anger appeared to give way to amusement. "Do you *want* to help me?"

I ignored his question. "Did you read the play?"

Now it was his turn to look sheepish. "Uh...yeah, I mean I tried, but I don't really understand it."

"Okay." I took deep breaths to help cool the heat in my face. "I can still meet you after school today, and we can go over it."

He nodded, a smug smile playing on his lips.

So, I'd screwed up, and now he was going to make the most of it. I looked away from his obnoxious triumph. "Sounds good."

A quick wave was all I could manage before I made my escape, but he wasn't going to let me go so easily. As I walked away, he called out, "Hey, but thanks for thinking about me, *Frances.*"

CHAPTER 6

Jesse

When I got to the library, Frances was already there, so we were both early. "Hey," I said, walking up to the table.

A smile touched her lips when she looked up, and her whole face looked different; it was lighter and soft. I willed myself to not stare like a creep and sat down, dropping my copy of the play on the table. "I swear I've been trying to read it."

"What were you doing, reading it in the bathtub?" she asked, inspecting the book's cover. The edges of the book were painfully dogeared, and the bottom was stained from a can of Mountain Dew I'd spilled on it when I fell asleep reading. "Good luck returning it to the library," she said.

"So, what did you think of the play so far?" she asked as she took out her notebook and pen. I had a feeling note-taking was something Frances did for fun.

"I think it's boring."

Her shoulders sagged. "Can you be more specific?"

What did she want from me? For a second, I wondered if it was too late to change my mind about that paper she wrote. "I guess Petruchio is pretty funny."

Her smile returned, and there was something else in her expression I hadn't seen before. Interest? "I agree, but what about Katherine?"

"She seems kind of crazy."

And her smile was gone. "Well, that's typical," she huffed. "You automatically label her crazy just because she doesn't willingly marry the first stranger to walk through the door."

I knew arguing might make her blow a gasket, but I realized I kind of enjoyed making her mad. "But she does marry him. So, why waste so much time being a bitch?"

She opened her mouth but closed it again. It looked like she was fighting some internal battle, when she finally said, "You said you didn't read it."

I folded my arms and leaned back in the chair. "I Googled it."

Considering my answer, she appeared to appraise me again, this time with less snark than before. "Have you thought about what angle you want to use for your paper?"

"What is there to write about? I mean, the play is like a million years old. It's not like I'm going to point out anything new."

"Not quite that old," she said. "I don't think Blackwell wants you to redefine Shakespeare. She just wants you to pick an angle and give an opinion."

Frances briefly ran through the major plot points of the story, but as she talked, I found my mind wandering to a different subject. "I saw what you did to Nick in the cafeteria."

She stopped talking and stared at me, but I couldn't tell if she was angry or not. I wasn't sure why I said it. Fumbling for something else to say, I added, "You really got him good."

She looked down at the book in her hands, but I didn't think she was reading. "Thanks, I guess."

"You don't care what people think about you, do you?"

"Most people are pretty disappointing," she said after a moment. "Why should I care what they think?"

I didn't know how to answer her, but felt like I knew what she meant. Blurting the first thing that came to mind, I said, "My dad cheated on my mom and got his girlfriend pregnant."

Again, she didn't answer, and the silence felt thick. Inwardly, I begged her to say anything.

"My mom's an alcoholic," she replied. "Since she came home

from rehab she's turned into the alcoholic Dalai Lama, and I can't stand her."

It took me a minute to register everything she said. "The alcoholic Dalai Lama?" I asked, fighting a threatening grin.

"It's an honorary title."

We both laughed, and the invisible barrier between us seemed to shatter. We laughed so hard, tears formed in her eyes and the corners of my face hurt. The girl at the front desk shushed us, but we ignored her.

When we finally got ourselves under control, her expression turned solemn again, but not as hard as before. "I'm sorry about your dad. He sounds like an asshole."

I nodded. "He is an asshole. The worst part is I don't totally hate him, even though I want to."

She nodded, as if she understood, and I had a feeling she did. After that, she passed her notes over to me and made some suggestions on angles to use for the paper. Neither of us brought up our personal stuff again, the wall between us firmly back in place. When it seemed like we'd both run out of things to say, I stood up and said, "Thanks for your help, Frances."

She cringed when I said her name, but didn't argue. I meant to just tease her a little, but my mouth went dry when she grabbed her bag, passed me a quick wave, and left without saying anything more. I followed a few minutes later, feeling confused. I barely knew Frances, so why did being around her suddenly feel so complicated?

CHAPTER 7

Frances

When I got home from school, Mom was in the kitchen balancing the phone against one ear as she took down notes for some benefit she was volunteering for. AA Mothers Against Laundry or something like that.

"Marsha, we have to get all the ice the night before and put it in the freezer because I won't have time to stop in the morning. Okay, great. No problem!"

She laughed at something Marsha said. I waved to get her attention, but she never looked up from her notepad.

The den was empty, so Dad was in his office, which was nothing more than a small closet under the stairs fitted with a desk and chair. The walls were plastered with photos of former students and game strategies scribbled onto scraps of paper.

I poked my head in and found Dad hunched over a pile of papers. "How does the lineup look for next year, Coach?" I asked, casually leaning on the doorframe.

"I've seen better, seen worse. I'm getting too old for this." He scribbled something into a playbook. "How was your day, Kitten?"

I shrugged. "Seen better, seen worse."

His forehead creased in concentration. Under the light from the single bulb dangling from the low ceiling, he looked older than I'd ever seen him. "Think we'll get dinner anytime soon?" he asked.

I glanced behind me and heard Mom's voice drift in from the

kitchen. If she was concerned about dinner, I was America's Next Top Model. "Dad, can I ask you something?"

He didn't look up from his papers. His glasses had slid to the end of his nose, threatening to fall off any second. "Shoot."

"Why did you stay with Mom?"

He stopped reading and looked at me. "What do you mean?"

I bit my bottom lip. We hadn't talked like this in a while. "I mean, after everything she put you through, why didn't you leave her?"

He slowly took his glasses off and placed them on the desk. His eyes looked sad, but when he spoke his voice was steady. "Because I love her."

Suddenly, I wanted to cry, but instead reached over and hugged him tightly.

He hugged me back and held my arms before I could pull away. "Is everything okay, Kitten?"

I nodded quickly, willing tears to not spill over my cheeks. I glanced over his shoulder at the papers on his desk. The varsity football roster was on top. "Hey," I said, grateful for an opening to change the subject. "Is Jesse on the roster?"

"Why do you ask?" he asked, taking the hint and putting his glasses back on.

"*Because,*" I said, "you asked me to help him write a paper so he can stay on the team. Why am I doing that if you were going to cut him anyway?"

"Do you think he'll follow through?"

I was startled by how sure I sounded. "Yes, I do."

He also looked surprised. "Okay, I don't have to make a decision until the new school year starts anyway, but I hope you're right about him."

Me too. "Thanks, Dad," I said, pleased by his willingness to trust my judgement. When I started to head upstairs, Dad called me back, and I poked my head around the corner. "Yeah?"

He gave me a long look over the rim of his glasses. "Do you like this boy or something?"

I rolled my eyes at him. "Dad, shut up." But on my way upstairs, I knew I hadn't given him an answer.

<hr>

OVER THE WEEKEND, Naomi and I were supposed to be working on her science project, but really, she was plotting ways to get Webb to take her to prom. She lay across her bed, cell phone in hand, prepared to dial his number despite all the rational arguments I'd presented to dissuade her.

"Franny, relax. This plan is foolproof." She had last year's yearbook open to Webb's picture.

"Foolproof is not how I'd describe this plan," I said. "Even if you convince him you're on the paper —which you're *not*— and successfully persuade him they want to do a story about his winning poem, which they *don't*, what does any of that have to do with prom?"

Naomi looked smug. "You let me worry about that, Franny." She slid a finger across her cell phone and keyed in Webb's number before I could protest further. "Hi, Webb? This is Naomi Lyons from school." Naomi nearly rolled off the bed with delight. "Anyway," she continued, "I don't know if you know, but I'm on the school paper this year. Oh? Well, I am."

I smacked my palm to my forehead and pretended to pull my hair out. *Oh. My. Hell.*

"I wanted to congratulate you on winning the poetry contest, and I wondered if I could interview you for a spotlight in the next issue."

There was a pause. I looked at Naomi and mouthed, "*Stop!*"

She grinned and waved me away. "Great! I'll check my schedule and get back to you."

Throwing my hands in the air, I mouthed, "*What schedule?*"

She covered the phone with her hand and said, "Shut up, I'm creating a mystery." She turned back to the phone. "I'll text you next week. Thanks, Webb. I look forward to working with you. What? How did I get your number?"

She turned around and shot me a panicked look. "Um...well, uh. I found it on Google. Yeah, well, you know, Big Brother and all. Okay, Webb. Thanks! Bye!" She quickly hung up, and we both squealed with laughter.

"You're insane. Again, how does conducting a fake interview with Webb translate to him taking you to prom?"

Naomi laughed off my concern as if she held a wealth of knowledge in human relationships. "Well, I have to get to know him first, don't I? I can't go to prom with just anyone. Besides, it's all part of the plan. I'll have him eating out of my hand soon enough." She closed the yearbook and grinned triumphantly.

"Uh huh. Right. How did you get his number, anyway?"

"Trevor jacked it from the volunteer clean-up sign-in sheet last semester."

"So, now you can add stalking as well as lying to your list of crimes." My tone came out sourer than I intended.

"Hey, something's up with you. You've been super negative all day."

"Have not," I argued, and turned away to grab my backpack. "Since we're not going to work, I need to get home."

Naomi circled me to catch my eye. "I know I'm right because now you won't look at me. What's going on?"

I opened my eyes wide in a sarcastic attempt to prove her wrong. "I'm looking at you, and everything is okay." But inside I silently cursed our long friendship.

"Did something happen while you were helping Jesse?"

"No," I said, feebly. "Why would you think that?"

She waited until our eyes met again before answering, and I was appalled by the pity I saw in them. "Franny," she said. "He's got a girlfriend."

"I know that." I scoffed, backing closer to the door. "What do I care?"

Naomi stared at me, and I forced a smile. "I've got to go." I walked out before she had a chance to say anything else.

CHAPTER 8

Jesse

"So, she wrote the whole paper for you?" Chris pulled his headset off one ear so he could hear me but kept one eye on his computer. *World of Warcraft* commandeered at least fifty percent of Chris's attention, but I had grown used to having broken conversations with him on guild nights.

His room was large but looked small because of an insane amount of junk thrown everywhere. Every surface was littered with dirty dishes, clothes, and old computer parts. Chris liked to gut computers and use the parts to make new systems. He was good at it too, but, unfortunately, his organizational skills were not as polished as his technical knowledge.

I sat on his bed and flipped through *The Taming of the Shrew* for about the hundredth time. Some of it was starting to make sense, which worried me. "That's what I said, isn't it?" I tossed the book down on the bed.

Chris growled into his headset. "Could I get a heal, please?" He covered his mic with his hand and glanced at me. "But she doesn't even like you. Why would she help you?"

"How should I know?" My cell rang, and Chris turned back to the game. I glared down at my dad's number as it pulsed on the screen. I sent the call straight to voicemail and slid the phone into my pocket.

"Wait, you think she was setting you up?" asked Chris. "No, not you, Britney, be right back," he said into the mic before covering it again. "It'd be just like her to plan some internal plagiarism sting operation. I'll bet she's working with the administration."

I rolled my eyes. "Don't be weird."

"It could happen," he said with a lopsided grin and turned back to the computer. "Okay, I'm back. Shut up, Travis. Can we do this, please? I need this armor to complete my set." Chris turned to me and muttered, "Amateurs."

Suddenly, the bedroom door flew open, and Lucy's slender silhouette stood framed in the doorway.

"Out," commanded Chris without turning to see who it was.

Chris's little sister looked like any normal twelve-year-old: blonde hair, pink leggings, and a boy band t-shirt. But underneath her preteen façade, Lucy was an evil genius who ran circles around her classmates and teachers. She didn't have many friends. Her parents said she had trouble relating to kids her own age.

Lucy's eyes narrowed at Chris before turning to me. "Mom wants to know if you're staying for dinner."

"I can't." I shoved my book into my backpack. "I've got to get home. Tell her thanks, though."

"Okay, you got your answer. Now get out," ordered Chris.

Lucy ignored her brother and stepped over a pile of dirty clothes she eyed with disgust. "I couldn't help but overhear your conversation."

"If by overhear, you mean listen at the door," accused Chris.

She shot him a classic little sister sneer. "The interesting part isn't that she wrote the paper for you, but why you didn't take it."

"It's really not that interesting," I argued.

"I've written loads of papers for you, and it never bothered you before."

I made an incoherent noise. "That's different."

She put her hands on her hips. "Seems to me you want this girl to think you're smarter than you really are."

I was beginning to understand why Lucy didn't have any friends.

"Thanks for that, but you're way off." I tried to walk around her, but she stepped in front of me.

"What's she like?" she demanded.

"Who?" Chris asked as he peeled one eye away from the screen.

Lucy rolled her eyes. "The girl, *stupid*."

"Frances?" I shook my head. Lucy was getting on my nerves. "She's...uh... I don't know... She's different."

She tilted her head. "In what way?"

I hesitated, unsure how to answer. It was a decent question. "In every way, I guess."

She flashed me a triumphant smile, as if I'd just proven her point. "You should give her flowers," she said. "Girls like flowers."

"Lucy, it's not like that. I have a girlfriend."

She waved her hand as if it were an unimportant detail. "Break up with her."

"Whoa, hold up. Be right back guys. I'll *be right back*, Dustin. Damn... Why don't you take this time to reset your bots so I don't die in the first five seconds next time?" Chris grumbled, "asshole" under his breath as he swung his chair around. "What the hell are we talking about here? Do you like Frances or something?"

"No, I *don't*," I said through clenched teeth. "And we're not talking about anything. I've got to go."

Chris shrugged and turned back to his computer. "What? No, I didn't call you an asshole. It must have been feedback. Whatever, Dustin. I take it back. You *are* an asshole." Chris waved at me as I walked out.

I didn't get halfway down the driveway before I heard my name. Lucy hung halfway through Chris's bedroom window, and I cringed when she yelled at the top of her lungs, "Don't forget the flowers!"

CHAPTER 9

Frances

"Don't forget to buy your prom tickets and make your final nominations before lunch. This is your *last* chance to nominate a prom king or queen," yelled Kevin Dias as he hovered protectively over a glitter-smeared ballot box. He and the rest of the prom committee had been peddling tickets and pushing people to make nominations all week.

I didn't bother to hide my annoyance as we passed the toilet-paper-adorned prom booth. At least after today I wouldn't have to listen to their obnoxious sales pitch anymore.

"Do you think anyone will nominate me?" asked Naomi.

I raised an eyebrow. A week ago, we'd all sworn off prom.

"Do you care? I mean, anyone can be nominated, but you know it'll be the usual suspects who win, so what's the point?"

Naomi shrugged and fell back against the locker with a sigh. "I know, I guess..." she trailed off as her gaze lingered longingly at the prom booth. "I just think it would be cool to be nominated, that's all. You agree, right, Trevor?"

Trevor nodded but didn't glance up from his history notes.

"Right," I said, nudging Naomi, "she said she wants to be the first woman to open a fro-yo on Mars. What do you think about that, Trev?"

"Yeah," replied Trevor, not looking at us. "That top looks great on you."

Naomi and I grinned at each other.

"*Anyway*," continued Naomi, "I just think it would be nice to know someone out there thought I deserved to be queen, you know? Even if I didn't win."

"Well," I said, "I'll nominate you if it means that much to you."

Naomi rolled her eyes and bumped my shoulder. "Thanks, but it doesn't count if *you* do it."

"If you say so. The whole thing is nothing but a desperate bid for attention, anyway."

Naomi's continued sighs of yearning told me she didn't agree. "Just thought it would be romantic."

"You think everything is romantic."

"I know," she grinned. "I'm lucky that way."

The bell rang, and Trevor put his notes away and came up for air. "What were we talking about?"

"Nothing important," I said, hoping to close the subject. But of course, Trevor just moved on to another I didn't like.

"Hey, Franny." He jabbed me with his finger, pointing down the hallway. "Your shadow is back."

I turned around just in time to see Sonny vanish behind a corner. Sonny's constant lurking had become hard to ignore. It was like being the focus of the saddest fan club in existence. My temper boiling over, I stomped down the hall and turned the corner after her. At first, I didn't see her, but then spotted a bit of neon pink backpack poking out from behind a row of lockers. I marched over, and she gave a tiny yelp of surprise when I stepped in front of her. Her thick brown hair covered her face, so only a single terrified eye stared at me behind the wall of hair.

"Why are you following me?" I asked.

Sonny moved off the wall and put some distance between us. She brushed at her arm, patting it two or three times as if some invisible hand had slapped her there.

"Well?" I demanded, advancing on her. Trevor and Naomi walked up behind me, but Sonny only gave a squeak of protest and began to tap the side of her head with her palm.

Her sudden panic made me question if confronting her was a good idea. "Hey," I said, softening my tone. "It's okay, don—"

But Sonny cut me off, yelling loud enough to vibrate my skull. "Newborn caterpillars' primary predators include birds, parasites, and spiders!" Without another word, she turned on her heel and ran in the opposite direction, leaving the three of us standing in the hallway wondering what the hell just happened.

As I MOVED from class to class, I couldn't stop thinking about Sonny. What was all that about spiders and caterpillars? I'd had a right to confront her, hadn't I? I thought so, but her frightened look, like a fly stuck in a spider's web, left me feeling guilty and defensive. By the time lunch rolled around, I was nursing a decent headache, too. I let my lunch tray drop on the table, and lasagna splattered everywhere.

"Hey!" demanded Trevor as he wiped a spot of tomato sauce from his shirt. "Do you mind?"

"Sorry," I sighed, sat down, and rubbed both my temples.

Trevor frowned. "Right, so why am I wearing your pasta?"

"Don't you have to change for gym next period, anyway?" I argued, my tone sullen.

Naomi wiped the table off with a napkin. "Still thinking about Sonny?"

I shook my head, hoping they would move on, but of course, they wouldn't.

"Do you think we really scared her?" asked Trevor.

Naomi's thin brows knit together. "She looked scared." Her quick agreement only darkened my mood.

"Could we talk about something else, please?" I asked, trying to ignore the throbbing in my head, but they ignored me.

"You could ask her," said Trevor. "She's right over there."

I followed Trevor's gaze to where Sonny, her back to a wall, inched along with her tray and glared at the floor as if it were lava. "Being Sonny," he added.

"What's she doing?" I asked.

"Your guess is as good as mine," replied Naomi.

"Hey, Sonny," called Trevor, and I slapped his arm.

"Ouch!" He batted my hand away. "What?"

"What are you doing?"

"Calm down, crazy. I'm helping. Our table could use some new blood." He gave me a pointed look that suggested I was being a jerk, which may have been true.

"Hey, Caterpillar! Come over here," Trevor called out again, and Sonny actually turned and looked at us.

Without hesitation, she headed straight for our table. *First, she runs away, and now just comes when you call her?* There was something about the way she walked: full speed without any evident awareness of the people around her. If someone were in her way, they'd best move if they wanted to avoid a full-on collision with a short, cat-eared girl on a mission.

Without being asked to sit, Sonny put her tray on the table and settled down without looking at us. She pulled an iPad out of her backpack and put on her headphones.

All three of us stared at her. She looked so absorbed that after a while, we gave up waiting for her to say something and continued our conversation.

Sonny counted chicken nuggets by sliding them into several segregated groups on her plate. What groups they might be, I had no idea.

Trevor leaned over and waved a hand in her face until she slipped the headphones off and looked at him.

"How did you get chicken nuggets? They said all they had was lasagna today."

"Some caterpillars consume twenty-seven thousand times their body weight in their lifetime," she responded.

I detected a slight note of annoyance in her voice, as if she thought Trevor's question had been a silly one.

"Okay. Good to know," he replied, and Sonny put her headphones back on.

Trevor nudged me and looked at Sonny. He was right. If I wanted to apologize, now was the time, but as I watched her slide her finger across the screen, I wondered if she'd even get what I was saying.

My window of opportunity was cut short when a shriek of microphone feedback sliced through the air. Everyone groaned and covered their ears, except Sonny, who blissfully focused on her iPad without interruption.

At the front of the cafeteria, Kevin looked apologetic as he tapped the microphone to get everyone's attention. The rest of the prom committee stood alongside him, one proud looking girl holding the glitter ballot box in the air. "Sorry about that, folks," said Kevin, "but it's the moment you've all been waiting for: the nominations for this year's prom king and queen!"

"Who's been waiting?" Trevor asked, loud enough for everyone to hear.

I grinned, but Kevin shot Trevor a dirty look before continuing. "The nominations, please," requested Kevin, and an enormously proud-looking girl in a cheerleading outfit handed Trevor the first slip of paper with a flourish. Kevin paused before belting out, "Lena Reeves for prom queen!"

A burst of applause erupted in the back of the room. Of course Lena was nominated. She was a tall, perfect goddess with silky black hair and flawless skin, who *actually stood* and took a bow while her friends cheered her on, fake surprise dripping off her face.

There were probably no other nominations for queen. Who would want to go up against Lena? It was no surprise when Nick Temple was nominated for prom king. Naturally, he yelled out some dumb remark about all his adoring fans.

My ears perked when they called Jesse's name. All the people at his table clapped and whistled, especially his girlfriend Sarah, but Jesse only shrugged, seemingly unmoved by the nomination. My face burned when I remembered our conversation in the library. Why had I told him all that stuff about Mom?

Kevin hesitated before reading the next nomination. He did a double take on the card, the name coming out like a question. "Frances Hughes?"

I didn't think it was possible for a room to go quiet that fast. For the next few seconds, the fast thudding of my heart was the only thing that cut through the dense silence. That is, until Trevor and Naomi both jumped from their seats and shouted a cry of victory worthy of the most bloodthirsty battles. Someone near Lena's table snorted a sarcastic, "Yeah, right," that was followed by moderate laughter to which Trevor so eloquently responded, "Oh, screw you!"

Recovering from the shock, I snatched Trevor's pant leg and yanked him back into his seat. Naomi sat down, too, but grinned so wide I thought her face might crack.

Glancing around the room, I was horrified to find almost everyone staring at me. But white-hot humiliation washed over me when my eyes connected with Jesse's, his lips slightly upturned in an amused grin.

Thankfully, after what seemed like hours, Kevin wrapped up his all-to-important nomination ceremony with calls for volunteers to help with prom decorating, and normal conversation resumed.

"Okay," I said, working hard to keep my anger in check. "Which one of you did it?"

Both my friends looked surprised. "I swear it wasn't me," Trevor blurted out, as if my evil eye had the power to melt him to goo. "Honestly, it wouldn't have occurred to me."

I turned my death glare to Naomi who *did* look guilty but also denied any wrongdoing. "I mean, I know we were talking about it," she said, "but I didn't think—" Suddenly, her expression brightened. "Franny, do you know what this means? Someone out there wants you to be prom queen! That is so roman—"

"No." I cut her off. "Don't say it."

Naomi looked like she wanted to argue, but that's when I noticed Sonny staring at me, headphones lowered around her neck. I couldn't read her expression, but it sure wasn't surprise. "Sonny?" I asked, "you didn't nominate me, did you?"

She stared at me for an infuriatingly long time without saying anything, so I asked her again, my voice beginning to sound a bit hysterical.

"The most obvious difference between queen and monarch caterpillars is that queens have three sets of tentacles and monarch's only have two," replied Sonny, in a tone suggesting that would clear everything up.

"What the hell does that mean?" I asked, but Sonny didn't answer and slipped her headphones back on.

Feeling overwhelmed by mortification and the ache in my head—which had now blossomed into full-fledged hammering—I turned to Naomi and Trevor. Both looked as dumbfounded as I was. "Does that mean she did, or didn't?" I demanded, but neither had an answer.

"Great. That's just perfect." I slammed both hands on the table as I got up to leave, but I didn't get halfway through the room before I heard someone behind me. I stopped, and Sonny, who had scooped up her iPad, backpack, and lunch tray crashed into my back. She dropped everything, including her milk, which spilled all over me.

Everyone laughed again, Sonny's eyes slowly traveled from the floor up to my face, reviewing the carnage. Her soulful expression looked desperate, begging me for the smallest bit of understanding, but in that moment, I had none to offer her.

"Leave me alone!" I yelled in her face before ditching my tray by the garbage and stomping out of the room.

CHAPTER 10

Jesse

Bleary eyed, I pushed the heavy locker room doors open. It had been a long day, and now I just had to get through gym before I could go home and crash. I'd caught my rhythm writing my paper around eleven the night before. By the time I checked the clock, it was already one in the morning. All I wanted was sleep, not rope climbing or running laps.

It didn't help that Chris would not shut up about *World of Warcraft*. "So, the trick is to grind the Purespring Elementals at the Swamp of Sorrows." He snapped his fingers. "The drop rate is pretty low, but if no one else is around you can kill enough mobs you can get an essence of water every few minutes."

"Sure, okay," I mumbled and shoved my bag into a locker. When it came to gaming, there was no way to steer Chris in a more interesting direction. You just had to ride it out until he finished.

While he listed off all the items needed to forge an imaginary sword, I caught a familiar name in a nearby conversation.

Nick Temple strolled in surrounded by his usual group of dudes who weren't good for much of anything except laughing at Nick's stupid jokes.

"She's had a crush on me since middle school, but she knows I wouldn't touch her, so she has to do pathetic stuff like pour drinks on me and nominate herself as prom queen just to get attention."

"Dude, you okay?" asked Chris.

I looked at him and realized I was gripping the locker. I slowly let go, pain radiating through my hand.

"I should just tell her," Nick continued, encouraged by the attention of the room. "It's not gonna happen. I guess I just don't have it in me to break her chubby little heart."

"You wish," said a snarky voice. It was the guy I'd seen sitting at Frances's table at lunch.

"Shut up, Trevor," said Nick, but with a flicker of hesitation. "We all know you have to stand up for your personal hag."

Everyone laughed, but Trevor crossed his arms and stared down his nose at them. The gesture made him seem older. "Frances thinks you're a joke, you know, but it's adorable how hard you try to convince everyone *you* don't like *her*."

Nick's jaw dropped, and his face ripened into a deep red. Some of the guys noticed and nudged him playfully. The idea that Nick might have a thing for Frances never occurred to me, and now that it had, I didn't like it at all.

"Whatever," Nick scoffed, his voice a little too high to be convincing. "You think I would touch that ugly fat bit—"

He didn't get any further because my forearm was jammed against his Adam's apple, and the only sound that came out was a strangled gurgle.

A couple guys tried to pull me off him, but it must have been for show, because they all fell away after a few tries. "What did you say about Frances? Try saying it now."

Nick's eyes bulged. His hands gripped my arm, and his former blush turned a deep purple until the shriek of Coach's whistle split the air like a guillotine.

I let my arm fall away, and Nick dropped to the floor in a pile of limbs, gagging and clawing at his throat.

"What the hell is this?" bellowed Coach as he charged into the room.

No one said a word, but I looked down at Nick. "Go ahead, tell him."

Nick glared at me, his hands still wrapped around his throat.

"Well?" Coach said. "I asked a question. Is someone going to give me an answer?"

Nick's voice was ragged, but he managed to croak out, "Nothing, Coach. We were just messing around."

Coach looked between me and Nick suspiciously. "Do we need to talk about this in my office?"

Nick coughed again. "No, Coach. Really. It's nothing."

Coach glowered at us, but only grunted in disapproval. "Change and get in the gym. *Now*," he said before stomping out.

I walked back to my locker, ignoring Nick as he snarled at his friends' attempts to help him up.

"Dude, what the hell was *that* about?" asked Chris. He tried to put a hand on my shoulder, but I shrugged it off. Chris raised both his hands in surrender. "Okay, Thor. Chill."

I closed my eyes and tried to let some of the tension drain out of me. When I opened my eyes, I sighed and rubbed my temple with the palm of my hand. I needed sleep.

Chris motioned to something behind me. Trevor stood there. He looked amused and something else. Smug maybe? "Jesse, right?" he asked.

"Yeah?"

"I've heard a lot about you," he said.

My adrenaline rush was fading fast, and I fought the urge to lay down on the bench and pass out. "Oh yeah? From who?"

Trevor ignored my question and offered me his hand. I stared at it for a second before taking it. Who the hell shakes hands anymore? Chris looked surprised, too, but returned the gesture good naturedly.

"So, I guess you're cooler than I thought," Trevor said. I tried not to be offended by the surprise in his voice. Before I could answer, he looked to Chris and asked, "Is he always this silent and brooding?"

Chris laughed. "Only since his billionaire parents were murdered by a street clown."

"Wow, a lot of that going around today."

"A lot of *what?*" I asked, even more confused.

"Brooding followed by extreme outbursts. Must be fate."

It seemed I was doomed not to understand because they both laughed again—too much if you ask me.

"Well," said Trevor. "I'll be seeing you."

I raised an eyebrow. "You will?"

Once Trevor was out of earshot, Chris's smile faded. "So, are you going to tell me what that was all about, or what?"

What did he mean about fate? I shook my head, too tired to think clearly. Besides, we still had gym to get through. "Or what." I rubbed a hand over my face. "Come on. Let's get this over with."

CHAPTER 11

Frances

I walked into school with the enthusiasm of a condemned woman. Everywhere I went it felt like people were staring at me. I tried to convince myself it was only my imagination, but that was hard to do when conversations all but stopped as I walked by. Class was worse. I could feel thirty sets of eyes boring into the back of my head.

Plus, there was no sign of Sonny anywhere. I hadn't handled things well, but now I was at least half-sure she was the one who nominated me. Whatever her intention, she'd managed to cause me a fair amount of grief in a short time.

I stopped by the art room before third period to talk with Trevor. I didn't like to admit it, but he dished out solid advice most of the time, and he usually managed to help extinguish my anxiety. That's why it surprised me when the first words out of his mouth were, "We need to come up with a plan to make you prom queen."

Slack-jawed, all I managed was an indignant, "Excuse me?"

"You're already behind as an unexpected nomination. We don't want to waste the advantage of being a surprise nomination by not having a solid campaign strategy."

Did he really think that was a reasonable answer? "Who cares about being prom queen? There's no way I'd win, anyway."

He frowned, placing both his hands on his hips. "Well, not with that attitude, you won't."

I took a deep breath and tried to count to ten, but Trevor's babbling about campaign meetings and brainstorming sessions forced me to give up after losing count two or three times. "Trevor, prom queens don't run campaigns; everyone just votes for who's popular."

Trevor cast me a look that told me how unsophisticated he thought my answer was. "Franny, please grow up. All queens campaign. They may not kiss babies or give speeches, but there are other ways of getting people's attention. Besides, you're more popular than you think you are."

I snorted. "Oh yeah? Says who?"

He ignored my question and brushed out the wrinkles in his shirt, looking official. "All in due time. Call it controlled chatter. As your campaign manager, it's my job to make sure information is released at the most opportune time."

Campaign manager? It seemed the one friend I counted on to be rational had completely lost his grip on reality. No. He'd loaded reality into a rocket and launched it to the moon. "No," I said firmly. "Whatever plan you've come up with, I'm not interested." I turned and walked away.

"Come on, Franny," he called after me. "You haven't even heard about my secret weapon yet!"

But I just waved and kept walking. No way would I become someone's pet project, especially since I knew it would come to nothing more than making me look foolish.

I tried to duck into the bathroom and nearly collided with two girls in a fit of laughter. We all stopped short, and their laughter died when they recognized me.

Lena Powell didn't exactly snarl at me, but she came close. It was more like the way someone reacts when they spot a cockroach running across the floor. "Excuse you," she said, her voice dripping with contempt as she pushed past me.

Her friend also cast me a smoldering look, and I rolled my eyes. *Perfect.* It appeared that the benefits of being nominated for prom queen were to begin immediately. *Where was a paper bag to wear over your head when a girl needed one?*

I pushed the bathroom door open but hesitated when I heard

someone crying. I didn't see anyone, but the pitiful moaning seemed to come from the handicap stall on the end.

"Uh...hello?" I said, but at the same time, I thought about retreating. Whatever had been going on here was none of my business, but the moment I convinced myself to leave, the sobbing upgraded to full-on wailing, and I sighed.

I knocked softly on the stall door, and it swung open slowly. What I saw looked like a horror film.

Sonny sat on the floor, pants around her ankles and legs spread wide over the tile floor. Her legs, hands, and face were covered in bright streaks of blood.

"Oh, my gosh," was all I could say as I dropped down to the floor beside her, but when I tried to touch her, she screamed and jerked away from me, eyes wild. Panic rose in my throat, and the sight of all the blood made me queasy, but I dug deep for calm, logic. "Sonny, are you hurt?"

I flinched against the fear in her eyes. Why should she trust me? I bit my lip until it hurt as I checked her over. Most of the blood looked dry and dark, and I couldn't find any cuts on her arms or face. "Sonny, please help me out here. Does anything hurt?"

She didn't say anything, but just when I was convinced she *couldn't* tell me, Sonny moaned and gripped her stomach tightly. My gaze fell to thick smears of dark blood on her inner thighs.

Oh.

I took a deep breath and tried to touch her arm, but again she pulled away and brushed her arm off as if my fingers burned her. There were red splotches of blood on her forehead where'd she tapped her head with the palm of her hand.

"Sonny, look at me."

She did, but streams of tears flowed down her cheeks, and she wailed in a sorrowful voice. "I'm dying."

"No," I said firmly, which caused her to start sobbing again. I glanced toward the door and frowned. "Did those girls tell you that?"

But Sonny only wailed and began to rock back and forth on the floor, whimpering the word, "mama" over and over.

I lifted my hands to my cheeks and closed my eyes, wishing I knew the magic words to calm her. "Sonny, listen to me. You are *not* dying. You got your period. It's normal." But as I said it, I heard how ridiculous it sounded. How do you explain how any of this was *normal?*

"I know it sounds nuts, but this happens to everyone—well girls, I mean." I stopped talking when Sonny's tense expression turned confused. If I wanted to make her understand, I was going to have to do it her way. "You know how caterpillars lay eggs?"

She didn't answer, but her sobbing slowed to small sudden bursts as she tried to catch her breath.

"Well, we have eggs too, but we don't lay them like caterpillars." How the hell did parents ever explain this to their kids? I tried to remember how my parents told me, but I was fairly sure that lesson had come from Google. "Well, bleeding is our bodies' way of saying our eggs are...uh...ready, I guess."

After a few more awkward rounds of the birds and the caterpillars, Sonny didn't appear comforted, but she stopped crying long enough for me to convince her to get off the floor. I handed her wet paper towels so she could clean herself up, and I dug in my bag, producing a maxi pad. I thanked every deity in existence that it wasn't a tampon because no way I was talking her through that one. She eyed the pad suspiciously but put it on, and I gave her my thin sweater to wrap around her waist.

We made a slow, silent march to the office, and when we walked in, the aide at the front desk took one look at us and went for the assistant principal.

Mrs. Finn was kind and listened carefully as I explained what happened, and I waited while they called Sonny's parents. Sonny sat like a statue, long paths of shiny tears marking her cheeks. I wanted to comfort her somehow but remembered how I'd screamed at her the other day and felt ashamed. In a way, I was no better than those girls in the bathroom.

After about twenty minutes, the office door flung open, and a short, stocky woman who looked to be in her seventies charged in. Her hair was gray and curled into a tight football helmet hairdo that looked like it required at least a hundred tiny rollers. She scanned the room with large, fierce eyes that looked just like Sonny's.

Sonny, who'd seemed unable to tolerate even the smallest physical contact, surprised me when she leaped from her seat and ran into the woman's arms, tears flowing all over again.

"*Qué pasó, mi amor?*" The woman cooed over and over while stroking Sonny's hair.

"Good morning, Ms. Reina," said Mrs. Finn as she stepped out from behind the desk. "It's nice to see you again."

I had been expecting one or both of Sonny's parents, but this woman was far too old. The woman only nodded briefly in acknowledgment, entirely focused on Sonny.

Mrs. Finn did not seem offended by this, and she calmly explained to Ms. Reina what happened. She gestured toward me. "This is Frances. She helped Sonny to the office and waited with her until you got here. Frances, this is Sonny's grandmother."

I winced internally when she said my name, but I managed to smile a little when Ms. Reina's eyes fell on me. She let go of Sonny and cupped both my cheeks in her hands, squeezing until my lips jutted out like a fish. "*Eres una buena chica,* Frances!" she said, and kissed both my cheeks several times.

Too surprised to react, I accepted all this affection without complaint. She wrapped her arms around Sonny's shoulders and led her to the door. Before they walked out, Sonny turned around and gave me a small wave, which I returned.

Confused, but feeling I'd won some small victory, I stared after them.

"Frances?" asked Mrs. Finn.

I forced myself to tear my eyes away from the door to look at her. Although she smiled, her tone was all business. "Are you okay?"

I only nodded in response and left the office. The sound of my footsteps echoed briskly off the walls, each step more determined than the last. The memory of Sonny's blood-streaked cheeks pressed me forward, boiling my temper so that by the time I made it to the cafeteria, I hit the doors so hard they swung open and cracked against the concrete walls. A bunch of students stopped eating and stared at me, but I only had eyes for Lena *Freaking* Powell.

She looked up just in time to see me slam my fist down on her table. Trays and drinks on the table shook and vibrated with the force of my anger.

Lena's eyes went wide. "What the *hell?*"

"You're going to pay for what you did," I said, and for a brief, satisfying moment, actual fear crossed Lena's face before she masked it with indignation. That was as good as a confession to me.

"I don't know what you're talking about," she replied, glancing around at her friends for support, but they all just stared at me. I doubted they'd seen anyone talk to Lena that way.

"Yes, you do," I spat at her, her lie making me want to grab the table and flip it on top of her. "Admit what you did to her."

"The girl in the bathroom? I didn't do anything to her!" Now that Lena had time to steel up her strength, she was all attitude. She stood up to meet my angry gaze at the same level.

"Well, you sure didn't *help* her. You just left her there, afraid. How would you like it if someone did that to you?"

Lena pressed her lips together, refusing to answer the question, but her eyes narrowed, and she hissed like a viper, "You can't do anything to me."

She wasn't wrong. Short of wiping the floor with her boney butt, and getting in a lot of trouble, there wasn't much I could do, but it was a temping thought. *Where were a pair of brass knuckles when a girl needed them?*

"You think you can do whatever you want." I pointed a finger in her face, "But I promise, you're going to learn what it means to lose. And if that doesn't work, you better hope I don't get a hold of some brass knuckles."

I was already walking away when I heard Lena say, "What did she just say?"

I headed straight for Naomi and Trevor, who sat wide-eyed, their mouths hanging open like everyone else. "Come on, Trevor," I said as I stormed past. "Let's talk about making me prom queen."

CHAPTER 12

Sonny

Most caterpillars protect themselves by mimicking colors in nature. They blend in with twigs or leaves, happy enough to munch their lives away while hidden from the world.

The rainbow caterpillar can't live this way. Its bright colors are impossible to disguise. Neon pinks, blues, and oranges shout, *I'm different from the others and I'm not afraid of you.* It's a trick, though. They hope predators will think their bright colors mean they're venomous, but they're really no deadlier than they are fearless. It's not as effective as looking like a leaf, but at least they don't pretend to be something they're not.

A boy bumped me in the hall. At my old school, there were arrows painted on the floor, and everyone stayed on their own side. Things were much easier there.

When our shoulders bumped, it felt like he hit me with a truck. He didn't stop or slow down, but whipped around and walked backwards away from me. "Hey, why don't you watch where you're going?"

I touched the sensitive spot where he'd hit me until the painful tremor that felt like pins and needles eased. His brows knit together in a look I knew well, the one that said I hadn't responded the way he'd expected. My papa used to tell me to smile at people when this happened, but I hadn't felt like smiling in a long time. The boy turned away.

Forty-six steps until I made it out of the main hallway, then another seventy-nine to the classroom. The noise in the hallway was oppressive. Voices echoed and hummed until I was sure my head would shatter, so I slipped my headphones over my ears. They didn't drown out the noise entirely but still gave me some relief.

Out of the main hall, it was easier to breathe. I wondered how other people could stand all the talking and bumping. No one worried about getting where they were going. Their lingering made me nervous, so I found quieter routes to class. Sometimes it made me late, but I never got detention. I wasn't sure anyone noticed, anyway.

Fifty-four steps to go. My stomached ached, and I gripped my bag. Inside were the pads *Abuelita* gave me to wear, but I hated the sight of the blood and its wet, sticky mess almost as much as I hated going back to the girl's bathroom. I preferred my own pink-tiled bathroom at home where my Hello Kitty toothbrush sat in a cup on the wall and the air always smelled like oranges.

Eight steps. Mr. Hernandez looked up from his desk and smiled at me. I nodded and dropped my bag on the floor by my desk.

Zero steps. Desks were arranged in a circle for our Life Skills class. Beside me, Dale sat drawing in a book with colored Sharpies. Dale didn't talk, which was why I liked sitting next to him. In the circle with us was Angie, Gigi, and Ricardo, but Ricardo liked to be called Rocky. Rocky wore a large hearing aid on the side of his head that made him look like a cyborg. Gigi had black hair tied into intricate braids that I couldn't stop staring at. Sometimes she'd scream when she was bored, and I'd have to put my head down until she stopped. Angie sat on my other side, clutching a stuffed dolphin under her arm.

"Do you know what my favorite sea animal is?" Angie asked, barely holding in her excitement.

I pointed to her stuffed dolphin, but she squealed and shook her head. This was the game. Every day Angie asked the same question, and no matter how you answered she always said no. But I was pretty sure it was the dolphin.

Mr. Hernandez liked to call us the Magnificent Five, but I didn't understand why. He walked around his desk and waved both hands in the air, like he did anytime he wanted our attention. "Now that we are all here, let's get started. Can anyone tell me what the next holiday is?"

"Valentine's Day!" yelled Gigi, followed by an excited giggle.

Rocky laughed.

"Wow, that's close, Gigi, but we celebrated Valentine's Day in February, remember?"

Dale raised his head from his drawing, and I could feel his eyes on me, but I wouldn't meet his gaze. On Valentine's Day, everyone in class exchanged small cards, but I forgot to tell Abuelita about it and didn't have anything to give. Dale passed out small store-bought superhero cards, but the one he gave me had five foil-wrapped candy ladybugs inside.

"What about you, Sonny?" asked Mr. Hernandez. I sank further into my seat. "Want to try to guess the next holiday?"

Everyone stared at me, and their looks felt like weights drawing my eyelids closed. I wanted to tell them that caterpillars didn't celebrate holidays, but it felt like too many words. "Prom?" I asked.

"Prom?" he looked surprised. "What a great guess, Sonny. I suppose prom does feel like a holiday, doesn't it?"

Rocky grinned and leaned back in his chair, both hands reaching behind his head.

"*I'm* going to prom, Mr. Hernandez," he bragged loudly. Rocky had a booming voice that hurt my ears. Normally, I would slip my headphones on when he was talking, but I was too interested to hear about his going to prom. It never occurred to me that any of us might go.

"You are?" replied Mr. Hernandez, prompting him. "Going with anyone special?"

"My girlfriend," boasted Rocky, his voice full of pride. "She goes to Trinity in Deltona."

"That's wonderful, Rocky. I hope you both have a wonderful

time." Mr. Hernandez looked around the room. "Anyone else have plans for prom?"

I raised my hand. It wasn't really a lie because I decided in that moment that it was true. I'd seen enough movies to know proms were full of loud music and people—both things I tried to avoid. But the way Rocky looked when he said he was going made me want to feel that way, too.

Mr. Hernandez smiled at me. "You're going to prom, too?"

I nodded, satisfied to see looks of envy on everyone's faces. I was going to prom. "With my friends," I added.

Mr. Hernandez went over more holidays with us. About fifteen minutes before it was time to leave, I glanced out the window and noticed a large orange tabby cat staring back at me. His expression looked annoyed, and I imagined if he'd had a watch, he would have glanced at it. I slid out from my desk and pulled my backpack around my shoulders.

Mr. Hernandez sighed. "Sonny, we've talked about this. You're not supposed to leave class before the be—"

But he was cut off by Gigi's high-pitched giggles. "She's doing it again, she's doing it again!" Everyone started laughing, except for Dale, who didn't seem to notice I'd left.

Forty-seven steps. I headed toward the emergency exit. It was usually locked, but the janitor stood holding the door for me. "He's been waiting for you," he said as I walked past him and out onto the school grounds.

The cat trotted over and rubbed himself between my legs. His fur felt like feathers gliding past my calves, and I ran my hand down the length of his back. From my bag, I produced a can of cat food and popped the top. He howled with delight at the sound.

Bill used a cinderblock to prop the door open and reminded me to shut it when I was finished. That was the deal: he opened the door, and I promised to close it. "Oh, and here is that wire you asked for." He left a small grocery bag of bendable cable by the door. "I hope someday you'll tell me what it is you're making."

Again, I didn't respond, and he didn't ask again before he left. Bill always knew when to leave.

The cat purred while he ate. He was fat, and eating made him happy. We sat in the parking lot until I heard the bell ring for lunch, and I gave him one more rub behind the ears. I slipped the cable in my bag and shut the door, testing it twice to make sure it was locked.

Sixty-one steps. The halls were full again, and I wondered if the boy who bumped me would come back this way. I put my headphones on as if they could shield me from harm.

Twenty-three steps. I hated the cafeteria. It was always loud and full of people walking in different directions. As if that wasn't enough, I stopped short on my way through the lunch line when I found a different lunch lady behind the counter. I pulled my headphones down and stared at her.

"You want pizza or hamburger, darlin'?" asked the lady in a thick southern drawl.

My limbs felt heavy. I had to force myself to blink to make sure I still could.

"You okay?" she asked, and there was that look again. It wasn't her fault, but I felt drained and exasperated because I couldn't explain how she was getting everything wrong.

Just when panic began to seize my chest, Ms. Adelle rushed in from the back of the kitchen, and I let go of the breath I'd been holding. She looked like the larva of an angel shade moth dressed in her starch white cooking jacket. Her black hair pulled tightly in a bun behind her hair net. "I got this," she said, as she reached into an oven and pulled out a warm tray of chicken nuggets.

The other lady stepped aside, and I automatically raised my tray so Ms. Adelle could dish out exactly twelve perfectly oval golden nuggets, no sauce. "Sorry about that, dear," she said with a wink. "She's new."

The other lunch lady looked confused.

"This one always gets nuggets. I have a supply in the back," she gestured to one of the freezers.

I waved at Ms. Adelle and continued through the line but not before I heard her say, "That one is special, but you won't find one sweeter. Not like these other hooligans." Her tone turned irritated as she yelled at a boy reaching his hand beneath the sneeze guard.

Part of me wanted to say I wasn't a child, but nuggets had been acquired, and I had somewhere important to be.

Seventeen steps. Trevor told me to meet everyone in the courtyard for lunch because they were having a secret meeting. I'd never been invited to a secret meeting before. No one seemed to notice when I got there, so I lowered my headphones around my neck so I could listen.

Frances looked mad. "Would you stop being so mysterious and just tell me what this secret weapon is?"

"Relax," Trevor said. "Once this gets out, it's definitely going to bring you some attention, but the less you know, the better. I wouldn't want the leak traced back to you."

Frances's mouth fell open, and I tilted my head, wondering if she knew there was a piece of lettuce stuck in her teeth.

"That does not make me feel relaxed. Whatever it is, I forbid it."

"You forbid it?" Trevor blanched, then he looked at me and smiled. "Did you hear that, Sonny? She forbids it."

I nodded. I'd heard it.

"Don't drag Sonny into this," snapped Frances.

I shifted my gaze between them, both locked in a battle like two monarch caterpillars in a fight over feeding territory.

"Can we please move on?" interjected Naomi. "We aren't getting anywhere by arguing. How are we going to get people to vote for Frances instead of Lena?"

"Sometimes caterpillars swarm to protect each other," I said, breaking the silence that followed. My cheeks felt hot, and I stared at the floor.

"Yeah?" said Frances, nudging Naomi. "You know, she's got an interesting idea."

Naomi blinked a few times. "She does?"

"Instead of trying to get people to vote for me *instead* of Lena, why not target people who generally wouldn't vote at all. You know, people like us."

"You got all that from swarming caterpillars?" asked Trevor.

"Think about it. There's no way Lena's friends will vote for me. So, we'll just increase the voting pool. You know, like when people go door to door registering people to vote before an election. We'll swarm 'em."

Frances looked at me, and my mouth twitched into a tiny smile. I liked being included in something where I didn't need to pretend to be something else.

"Well," said Trevor, looking thoughtful, "I could talk to one of the guys on the student paper, see if they could get the word out. People might be interested to know there's more than one kind of queen out there. Naomi, you have an in at the poetry club. Why don't you get your new boyfriend to drop Frances's name and see if we can get a few bites?"

Naomi frowned. "He's not my boyfriend. I mean...not *yet*, but I doubt the poetry club is that interested in who gets crowned prom queen."

"Well, that's the point, isn't it?" insisted Trevor. "You've got to make them interested."

They all talked so fast my mind drifted. I imagined a set of large colored wings unfolding. Their bright rainbow colors shining brightly in the dark, attracting everyone around them closer. I would do anything to see them become real. I just hoped everyone didn't think they were toxic.

CHAPTER 13

Frances

The day after the first meeting of what Trevor had dubbed, "Operation Crooked Crown," I walked home from school a ball of nerves. What had I gotten myself into? After confronting Lena in the cafeteria, I began to wonder if challenging her was just another example of my temper getting the better of me. Who was I kidding? No matter how many people we talked to, there was no way I was going to be crowned prom queen, and even if I did...what then?

My phone vibrated in my pocket. I wasn't in the mood for another of Naomi's hourly Twitter updates, so I ignored it.

Another question still lingered like a dull ache: Why had I confided in Jesse? I tried not to picture him joking about my screwed up family with his friends but failed. Needing to take a step back from the emotional cliff in front of me, I closed my eyes and took several deep breaths as I walked. I was being silly. Chances were he'd already forgotten our conversation, but for some reason that made me feel even worse. I opened my eyes when my phone buzzed again and once more, I ignored it. *Where was some peace and quiet when a girl needed to wallow?*

I walked by our neighbor Ms. Weary as she watered rows of yellow roses along the fence line that separated our yards. She had a pinched face with a frown cemented into a wrinkled expression. I waved, but she cast me a suspicious look in return as I made my way up the drive. I rolled my eyes and went inside. *Typical.*

The television in the den was on. Two half-bald heads hovered above the couch. Mom, as usual, was nowhere to be found.

"Hey, Kitten," called Dad.

"Hey, kiddo," parroted Bill a second later. Neither bothered to look away from the football game. "Dump anymore drinks on people's heads today?" teased Bill. "I admire your fire, kid, but remember, I'm the one who's got to clean up the mess."

"Sorry, Bill," I said. "I'll try to be more considerate." I trudged upstairs, indulging in a few moving-out-of-the-house-the-moment-I-turn-eighteen fantasies.

My cell buzzed again, but this time I admitted defeat and looked at it, now ready to welcome a distraction from my gloomy thoughts. I had seven missed calls from Naomi and five text messages. I listened to the first message:

"Franny, you have got to call me. You're never going to believe what's going on. Oh my *heck*. Call me!" Her voice was a peculiar mix of hysterical delight.

The second message, left only a few minutes later, sounded even more frantic. "Why the *hell* aren't you picking up? Did Trevor talk to you? Because he promised he would let me tell you. Call me back!"

Confused, I checked my text messages and found more of the same from Naomi, but there was also a message from Trevor.

Secret weapon activated was all it said, and my stomach fell below my knees.

There was a separate group text where Trevor had sent a YouTube link to about forty other numbers. Did we even know that many people? I clicked it with a shaky finger. The video was impressively clear. I recognized the locker room outside Dad's office, and I raised an eyebrow when I saw Nick.

"Whatever," Nick said. "You think I would touch that ugly fat bit—"

Then suddenly, there was Jesse. "What did you say about Frances? Try saying it now."

I sprung off the bed. Did he just say what I think he said? It all happened so fast. After rolling the video back, I watched the scene play out again, transfixed as three guys tried and failed to pull Jesse off of Nick. Then a whistle, and the video ends.

My head swam, and I slid my finger across the screen to watch it again and again. *Why would he do that?*

Trevor had shared the video everywhere, tagging me on Twitter, Instagram, and Facebook—including our school Facebook page. I slowly sank back down on the bed. Shock, dread, and something unexpected—maybe excitement—made all of my nerves stand on end. The number of views was already well into the thousands

CHAPTER 14

Jesse

I smashed the snooze button on my alarm more than once. Even though I'd crashed early, I still hadn't made up enough sleep from my all night writing session to get me out of bed on time. Eventually Mom came in and demanded I get ready for school. I cursed when I realized I'd forgotten to charge my phone, and it was long dead. My body felt like it weighed a ton as I rolled out of bed and dragged myself into the bathroom. I hoped a shower would wake me up. It didn't.

The final bell rang just as I got to school, and I had to dash to my locker. Most of the hallway was clear, so when I closed my locker door and Sarah's face suddenly appeared behind it, I jumped.

"Sarah. Hey." I forced a tight smile, but she gave me a dark look. *Uh oh.* I ran through a catalog of things I could have done wrong, but nothing obvious came to mind. "Everything okay?"

"No, Jesse. Everything is *not* okay."

When she didn't continue, I sighed. Great. Whatever I'd done, I was supposed to know what it was. That was never good. I scrambled for a response. "Yeah, uh, sorry I didn't call last night. I was pretty tired."

Her angry look told me that wasn't the problem, but I probably didn't win any points by pointing it out that I hadn't called.

"We need to talk." She snatched my shirt sleeve, yanking me into a small alcove at the end of the hallway. She whirled on me so fast I had to duck her ponytail before it hit me in the face.

"I want to know what's going on," she demanded.

"What are you talking about?"

She pulled her phone out of her purse and shoved it in my face. "This is what I'm talking about."

I took it from her and was stunned when I saw a video of Nick and I in the locker room. The scene from yesterday played out in front of my eyes. "Wow," I said, a slight grin forming. "It's got a lot of views."

She snatched the phone back. "Really? That's all you have to say?"

I sighed, weariness creeping over me again—or maybe I was only tired of her. "Sarah, what do you want me to say?"

"How could you do this to me?"

"Do *what* to you?"

"This is so humiliating." Her voice dropped to a soft whine. "*Everyone* is talking about you guys."

"Who cares? You don't even know Nick Temple."

"Not Nick, you *jerk*," she snapped, punching my shoulder.

"Ow." I rubbed my arm. For a cheerleader, she had a nasty right hook.

"Everyone is talking about you and Frances." Tears welled up in her eyes. "You've never defended *me* that way."

I shifted my weight around. Was I supposed to feel guilty about this? "I'm sorry, okay? Nick was being an asshole, so I gave him a hard time. That's all it was." But as the words came out, they had an untruthful ring to them.

She gave me a sullen look. Had she always looked like this when she was angry?

"Come on, Sarah, don't be that way. I bet you'd like Frances if you got to know her," I offered weakly, but the words hung awkwardly in the air. Now that I said it, I couldn't imagine Frances and Sarah ever hanging out.

A biting, sarcastic laugh escaped her lips. "No, thank you, and I want you to promise me you won't hang out with her either."

Surprisingly, I didn't have to think about it. "I can't do that."

"Then maybe we don't need to see each other anymore," she said, her chin jutting out in defiance.

I tensed at her threat but refused to cave to her stupid demand. "Maybe we don't."

She gawked at me, her outrage crumbling into hurt and shock. "But what about prom?" she asked, her voice dropping below a whisper.

There it was: the whole reason we stayed together. All she wanted was a limo and a stupid prom picture that she could dress up for. "I'm sure you won't have a problem finding someone else to go with."

Her lip quivered for a second before she screamed "*Fine!*" into my face, turned on her heel, and ran down the hall.

I stared after her, feeling numb and exhausted again. Someone cleared their throat behind me.

The school janitor leaned in the doorway of his office. He was a tall, thin guy with an angular face and worn t-shirt with the school's logo on it. "I didn't mean to eavesdrop," he said, "but you guys were loud."

"Yeah, sorry," I said. "It's just, well, you know." I gestured in the direction Sarah had run. What more was there to say?

The janitor grinned and pulled a Red Bull out of his back pocket. "Women."

As if the day hadn't been wonderful enough, an aide walked into history class to haul my butt to the office. When Mr. White called me to the front of the room, a few whispers and giggles told me most people already suspected what it was about.

"They need you in the office, Jesse." His tone wasn't judgmental, but it wasn't sympathetic either.

I took the slip and followed the aide to the office. If she knew anything, she wasn't talking. It had to be about the fight. What's the worst that could happen? Detention? Suspension? It's not like I could deny what happened. The last time I checked, the video had almost 15,000 views, and someone had tagged both me and Nick.

When we got to the office, the aide discarded me in front of the principal's office. Signaling me to wait, Mrs. Finn walked into the office then held the door for me to go in.

"Thanks," I muttered as I passed her.

Principal Morel sat at his desk, but I froze when I saw Mom seated in one of the chairs, the skin around her eyes red and puffy. A pang of guilt hit me in the chest, and I officially started to worry.

Nick was there too, sitting next to a woman I assumed was his mother.

I took the empty chair next to Mom without being told.

"Good afternoon, Jesse," said Morel. His tone was too cheerful for the situation, but at least he wasn't yelling. "How are you today?"

"Uh, been better, I guess."

Morel frowned, and Mom gave me an irritated look, which I returned with a "what?" expression. What did they want from me? Were they really looking for the low-down on my day?

Morel gestured to Nick and his mom. "I believe you know Nick. This is Mrs. Temple."

I nodded in response, afraid I would make things worse if I spoke again.

"I take it you know why we've called this meeting."

I nodded again, so he continued. "We'd like to discuss the incident that took place Monday. Assault is a serious matter. Not only is it a crime, but we have a zero-tolerance bullying policy. Violence of any kind severely disrupts the peace and enjoyment of the school for others. Students have a right to attend classes and school functions without the fear of bodily harm."

Bullying? I tried to keep my expression fixed, but my heart pounded inside. *Holy crap, is that what I am?* I peered at Mom for help, but she just stared at Morel, her face grave.

"Then there is the separate issue of a highly circulated YouTube video." Morel looked at Nick's mom. "We have contacted YouTube several times to have the video removed, but it's a process."

Nick visibly stiffened at the mention of the video. His mom put her hand on his arm, but he jerked it away.

Morel watched this exchange and sighed. "You wouldn't happen to know who took that video would you, Jesse? Or who posted it?"

"I don't know. I mean...I didn't even know there was a video until this morning."

Morel nodded, but Nick's mom looked unconvinced. "Well, he's certainly not going to admit to it now," she accused.

"I didn't post it." I kept my eyes forward.

Mom put a hand on my arm, and the knot in my stomach unclenched a little. At least she believed me.

"Well, that's good to hear, Jesse," said Morel. "I would hate to think you actively took part in any form of cyber bullying on top of what has already transpired. I'd like to stress to you how very lucky you are."

I raised an eyebrow. This should be good.

"So long as you apologize, Nick's parents have agreed to allow the school to come up with a suitable punishment rather than contact the authorities."

Apologize? Mrs. Temple stared at me, and I glanced at Mom. She looked tired, and a fresh wave of guilt washed over me. *Damn it.*

Nick looked green and miserable, and it occurred to me that he probably didn't want to be there any more than I did. "I'm sorry," I said, surprised it was true. Nick *was* a jerk, and I'd wanted to put him in his place, but having a video of what happened floating around was like pouring salt in a wound. "And I'm sorry someone recorded it," I added as an afterthought.

In that moment, I remembered Trevor's easy introduction the other day, and I clumsily reached between our chairs to offer Nick my hand. At first, he glowered at it, but his mom nudged him, and he begrudgingly shook it for half a second before letting it drop.

"Fine," he muttered, and looked away.

I sat back in the chair and looked at Mom. She didn't smile, but her expression had softened considerably.

"Wonderful," continued Morel. "Although there won't be legal charges, there is still the matter of punishment. Jesse, you will be suspended for a week. Upon your return, you are to complete twenty hours of community service here at school."

I leaned back in my chair. Okay, that didn't sound too horrible.

"And since our sports program has a zero-tolerance violence policy, you will be ineligible to play football for at least one year."

"*Seriously?*" I looked between Morel and Mom, but the look on their faces told me it was no joke.

"If you behave yourself and there are no further incidents like this over the next year, you can try out again," said Morel, already gathering the papers on his desk.

"But I'll be a senior next year," I argued, my voice rising. "I was supposed play varsity."

"Well, you should have thought of that before you decided to bully other students," snapped Mrs. Temple.

"That's total bull," I said, almost yelling. I knew it was pointless. This had already been decided before I'd walked in, but I couldn't help it. "*He's* the one who bullies everyone. Where the hell is *his* punishment?" The realization that I would not be allowed to take the field again hit me all at once, and I rose from my seat. Mom grabbed my forearm and yanked me back down.

"Jesse, enough!" she said, her voice cracking.

I glared at her. It's a good thing they told me this after the apology.

"So, if there's nothing else you ladies would like to add," said Morel, ignoring my outrage, "let's consider the matter resolved. I hope we can all move forward in a more positive manner from now on." Morel shot me a stern look, and I had to fight the urge to tell him what he could do with his positive manner.

"I think we are satisfied, Mr. Morel," said Nick's mom as she picked up her purse.

"Thank you for everything," said Mom. "Let's go, Jesse."

As we left, I felt a tension between Mom and Mrs. Temple that I hadn't noticed before. Mrs. Temple frowned, and I got the feeling she'd expected Mom to say goodbye or apologize. It didn't happen, and I couldn't help but feel a little satisfaction as we walked out of the office.

"You can wipe that smile off your face," Mom said as we walked down the hall. "You're in big damn trouble." She moved so fast I practically had to run to keep up with her. Without stopping or looking at me, she held out her hand. "Phone."

I had never been in this much trouble before, so I had no idea what to expect from her. I handed over my phone, and she dropped it into her purse. I wondered how many years it would be before I saw it again.

She was silent until we were halfway home, but I felt the storm coming.

"Is it because of the divorce?" she asked. "Are you trying to get our attention?"

I stared at the car ceiling, my words flowing out in a long, exasperated sighs. "No, Mom. This is not about you and Dad."

"Well, Jesse, I don't understand. What would possess you to put your hands on another person like that? I mean, you were choking him. You could have been arrested. Do you have any idea what it was like for me to watch a video of you hurting another person?" A tear rolled down her cheek.

I cringed. *Why was she taking this so personally?*

"Is this about the girl you were talking about in the video?"

I could feel my face flush, and I glared out the window.

"Jesse, showing off for some girl is no excuse for this kind of behavior. What you did was wrong."

I wanted to stay calm, but after everything that'd happened— Sarah, the video, being kicked off the team—all my nerves lit on fire.

"I wasn't showing off," I said through clinched teeth. "Not *all* guys are assholes like Dad."

To that gambit, she said nothing until we were parked in the driveway. Both of us just breathed in the rising temperature of the car.

"Jesse, I know you're angry with your father, and so am I, but you know he's never hit anyone. If you want to be mad at him, that's okay. But do not use him to excuse your mistakes. You made a choice to put your hands on someone, and you sure didn't learn *that* from your father."

She was right. Dad never hit me. He never hit anyone. He always wanted to talk things out, but I just couldn't bring myself to say anything nice about him. "Whatever," I said and got out of the car.

CHAPTER 15

Frances

The following Monday I tried to avoid all contact with humans. No one dared mention the video except for Naomi, who refused to talk about anything else. Everywhere I looked people had their heads down, laughing, their gleeful attention directed to their phones. It had to be in my head, right? People were always looking at their phones. It didn't necessarily mean they were watching the video. Sadly, the more I repeated this mantra, the less convincing it sounded.

When I got to my locker, a sudden quietness shrouded the hallway. Trevor was already there, grinning like a fool, and several violent scenarios ran through my head. Of course *he* would be happy about all this.

"Well, if it isn't our little celebrity," said Trevor way too loudly.

"Shut up, Trevor," I said, irritated by his lack of discretion. "I could kill you for this."

He feigned a wounded look. "Me? Oh, come on Franny. We needed a way to get you on everyone's radar. Well, thanks to Harmon, mission accomplished." He gestured around, and my eyes followed. People gawked at us as they walked by. Most looked as shocked as I was while others only smiled slyly as if we shared a secret. I just wished I knew what it was.

"Anyway, you never would have believed me if you hadn't seen the video for yourself. I mean, he nearly slayed Nick in your honor."

"Stop exaggerating," I snapped. "Why didn't you just show the video to *me*? You know it's got over twenty-five-thousand hits now?"

Trevor chuckled. "And how many of those are yours?"

"I just feel like everyone is laughing at me," I said, sidestepping his stupid remark.

"Franny," he said, his tone slightly more delicate, "I know this is hard for you, but we needed this boost. Now that people know who you are, they can start to know you're worthy to be queen. Anyway, everyone is laughing at Nick, not you." Trevor peered around the hallway. "By the way, have you seen him? I don't think he had the stones to come in today and face the music."

"No." But I didn't have much time to think about Nick because Naomi bounded toward us, a huge smile plastered across her face.

I immediately held up my hand. "I don't want to talk about it."

Her smile transformed into a pout. "But Franny," she whined, "I got some juicy gossip to tell you."

"I don't care. From now on, I don't what to know about anything and I don't want to talk about anything."

Naomi looked from me to Trevor and stamped her foot. "But this is primo stuff I got here." She leaned in close as I tried to open my locker, her smile widening. "It's about Jesse."

I schooled my face. "So?"

"Well, if you don't want to know, I guess I won't tell you."

Naomi had been baiting me this way since elementary school. It didn't work then, either. "Fine, don't tell me."

I cast her a smug look and ignored her reddening face. She lasted about fifteen seconds before she blurted it out. "Jesse broke up with Sarah."

She officially had my attention.

Even Trevor looked shocked. "Are you kidding? Quarterback breaks up with cheerleader? That *is* big news. What happened?"

"*And...*" she continued, almost salivating on the meaty gossip, "he got suspended."

I gaped at her. "All that happened today?"

"Friday. Bianca Johnson told me Sarah was in the ladies' room after first period on Friday, crying because Jesse dumped her right in the middle of the hallway. Later, Linda saw Jesse walking out with his mom."

I put my hands over my face, my head swimming. "This is all my fault."

"No," said Trevor firmly. "He probably broke up with Sarah because he finally figured he could do better. As far as getting suspended," Trevor paused, "if it's anyone's fault, it's mine. If I hadn't posted that video..." he trailed off. "Damn. I didn't think he would get into *that* much trouble. I mean, your dad broke it up before anything really bad happened. Why would the school make such a big deal about it?"

"Just forget it, okay?" I said, feeling overwhelmed. "Can we please talk about something else?"

"But this is the most exciting thing that's happened in a long time," Naomi persisted. "How can you not want to talk about this?"

"Let it go, Naomi. She's in overload," interjected Trevor.

"All right," she said. "Well, I've got my interview with Webb this afternoon. Can we at least talk about that?" She leaned against the locker and pulled out a spiral notebook. "You guys want to hear the questions I'm going to ask him?"

"You mean the fake questions for the fake interview for the newspaper you don't actually work on?" I didn't bother to curb my judgmental tone. If she wanted me to humor her, she was going to have to pick a different day.

"Will you keep your voice down, please? Anyway, quit being so negative. So far, my plan is working perfectly."

"All your plans work perfectly," Trevor pointed out, "until they don't."

"Cut it out!" She smacked his arm.

I tried to stay present in the conversation, but my mind kept drifting to Jesse. Why would he pick a fight with Nick over me? Just because I helped him with his paper? Whatever his reasons, I was sure he must regret them now.

"Hello? Franny, are you listening?" asked Naomi.

"Nah," said Trevor. "She's worrying."

"We were talking about Webb." I cast Trevor a dark look.

"Anyway, so question four," continued Naomi. "If you could be any character in the Harry Potter series, who would you be?"

I blinked at her. "What kind of question is that?"

"Harry Potter happens to be a very relevant piece of pop culture that helped define our generation."

"First of all," said Trevor, "he's going to know that's a phony question. Second, if anything, it defined our parents' generation."

"What if he hasn't read the books?" I added.

"Then we can watch the movies together when we're married." She sounded so sure of herself, it was a little scary.

"Question five: who is your favorite Avenger?"

"Captain America," replied Trevor instantly.

Naomi smirked. "You just like him because he's the hot one."

"Oh, Naomi." Trevor put an arm around her shoulder. "That's why everyone likes him."

"Are any of these questions related to Webb's poetry?" I asked. "Isn't that why you're interviewing him in the first place?"

She looked at me, her face blank. "You think I should throw in a poetry question to make it seem legit?"

"Have you even read his winning poem?"

"Well, not exactly."

"Don't you think he'll find it odd that you're interviewing him for winning the poetry contest and you haven't even read the poem? I think there is a copy posted on the wall by the teachers' lounge."

"Oh, you're right!" Naomi reached over and gave me a quick hug before she bolted, yelling a thank you behind her.

Trevor looked at me and grinned. "To be in love."

AFTER THE NORMAL routine of dinner and homework, I retreated to my room for some much-needed solitude. The moment my bedroom door clicked shut, I slid to the floor and closed my eyes against a wave of tension. Why did I care what happened to Jesse, anyway? It's not like I'd asked him to defend me. Still, knowing that he did only tightened the knot in my stomach. My phone rang, and I willed my heavy hand to pull my phone out of my pocket. "Hello?"

I was greeted with Naomi's long, satisfied sigh. "His favorite Harry Potter character is Snape."

I smiled and allowed my gloomy thoughts to fade into the background. Snape was Naomi's favorite character, too. "Must be destiny."

"Don't be sarcastic, Franny," she said. "I'm in love."

"I take it he bought the whole newspaper ruse?"

"Completely." I could hear the smile in her voice as she talked. "He's even more interesting than I imagined. Did you know his dad died when he was six years old?"

"That's horrible."

"I know," she swooned. "He's such a tortured soul."

I rolled my eyes. "So, did you ask him?"

"No, I have to meet with him a few more times before I can trick him."

"Is the goal really to *trick* him?"

"Oh, Franny, how little you know about these things."

"Right," I said. There was a loaded pause, and I could feel the subject change coming.

"So," she said. "Are you ready to talk about it yet?"

"Nope."

"Franny," Naomi said, using her careful voice. "I know you feel bad about Jesse getting in trouble, and maybe he didn't handle things the right way, but I'm glad he stood up for you. You're a great person and deserve to be defended."

I knew she wanted to make me feel better, but I couldn't think of a single thing about me that made that statement true. "Thanks, but I don't need defending, and I don't care what Nick or any of his stupid friends think."

"But maybe you care what Jesse thinks?"

I jumped at a sudden knock on the door. No one ever came up to my room. "Yes?" I called out.

"It's me, Kitten," replied Dad's gruff voice from the other side of the door.

"Got to go. Talk to you tomorrow." I ended the call as I stood up, not entirely unhappy to cut the conversation short.

When I swung the door open, Dad peered around like he was entering a forbidden tomb or a church sanctuary. I couldn't remember the last time he'd come up here.

"What's up?"

He gingerly made his way over to my bed and sat down. The bed flattened under his weight. His serious expression alarmed me. "Is it Mom?"

"What? Oh, no, she's fine," he said, but gave me a level look. "I think we need to have a talk." When I didn't respond, he continued but didn't seem happy about it. "There's a video floating around, and some parents complained."

"I already know about it." I felt silly I hadn't considered this. Of course Dad would know all about it. "You didn't get in trouble, did you?"

"Not really." He cleared his throat. "But now I have to write an incident report every time something like this happens. Extra paperwork, but...that's not what I want to talk about."

"Okay," I said warily.

"Bill showed me the video and, well, at the time I didn't know what they were fighting about." He paused, looking ashamed and unsure how to continue.

I tried to help him along. "And now that you do?"

He smiled slightly, but his eyes were lined with worry. "I just want to make sure you're okay."

I smiled back, uncomfortable, but touched by his concern. "Don't worry, Dad. Those guys don't have the power to shake me up."

Without warning, his large arm shot out and curled around my shoulders. "That's my girl."

When he let go, he asked, "Now, is there something else you want to tell me?"

I raised an eyebrow. "Such as?"

His smile disappeared. "Like something about you and Jesse Harmon? Because I'm going to be honest, Kitten. I'm not sure I like that idea."

"There's nothing to tell," I said too quickly, my cheeks burning.

He grunted and seemed to sense I wasn't telling the whole truth, but what could I say when I didn't know what the truth was?

"Well, when I was his age, boys didn't get into fights about chicks they didn't like."

I choked back a laugh. This conversation was turning even more shades of mortifying than I could have imagined. "Well, they don't call them 'chicks' anymore, but honest, Dad, I just helped him with his English paper. That's it."

"Well, that's the other thing. I'm not sure it matters anymore because Jesse was removed from the football team."

I stared. "He got kicked off?" No one had mentioned that this morning.

Dad shrugged. "The athletic program has a zero-tolerance violence policy."

All the atoms in my body screamed against it, pushing me to argue. "But that's not fair! He didn't really hurt him, did he? Isn't there anything you can do?"

Obviously, Dad wasn't as upset as I was, but at least he had the decency to look solemn. "Sorry, Kitten, but it's out of my hands."

Not only had Jesse and his girlfriend broken up, but he'd been suspended and kicked off the football team all in the same day. When I didn't say anything, Dad stood up. "Well, I have some work to do. You sure you're okay?"

I wasn't but nodded anyway.

He let his hand rest on my shoulder for half a second. "Mom should be home soon. Would you like me to send her up?"

"What for?" I asked in a clipped tone.

After a moment's hesitation, he replied, "Nothing, never mind," and left the room.

When he closed the door, I sighed and let myself fall back on the bed. I could tell my answer disappointed him, but I was too angry to care.

CHAPTER 16

Jesse

On my first day back after suspension, I had to stop by the office to get a pass for first period. The office assistant let me know that I was to report to the janitor's office after school to start my "community service." Even though I was being forced into hard labor, I still preferred it to being at home. The tension between Mom and I had been thick over the last week. Not that I had a lot of time to sit around and worry about it. Between the overlapping streams of lectures and chores, she made sure I didn't have much down time. My only reprieve was when I was working on my paper. Even though finishing it wouldn't get me back on the team, writing helped keep my mind off all the problems that waited for me when I got back to school.

Without thinking, I walked to my usual table at lunch but stopped short when only Chris was sitting there. I put my tray down and looked at him. "Where is everyone?" I asked, afraid I already knew the answer.

Chris shrugged. "Defectors to the Empire. Travis and José's girlfriends are Sarah's friends, so they're barred from fraternizing with you." He pointed his forkful of mac and cheese in the direction of a nearby table.

Sarah sat surrounded by a cocoon of her friends. They noticed me looking and hissed like a pack of angry badgers. Travis and José cast me apologetic looks but turned away.

I sighed and sat down. "So, we're the Rebel Alliance and Sarah is...what, the Empire?"

"Nah, the Empire is all of womankind," Chris said. "Sarah's Darth Vader."

Suddenly I wasn't very hungry.

Chris leaned back and watched me. "Hey, man, don't worry about it. I always said you would be better off without her. She's a blank." He knocked on his head. "Nothing between the ears, you know?"

I shrugged, relaxing my shoulders with a sigh. "I'm not upset about Sarah. I just wish they hadn't kicked me off the team."

Chris waved his hand as if it was old news. "Forget the team. We don't need them, anyway."

I nodded, but then his words sunk in. "What do you mean *we*?"

He shrugged. "I quit the team. No way am I going to stay after they kicked you off. Let Coach find a way to replace us both next season."

Chris and I had been friends for a long time, but I never expected him to quit the team for me. It made me wonder if I'd do the same for him. "Thanks, man, that's...really cool of you."

"I know," he said with a grin. "I'll have you know, I'm a pretty cool guy."

After a glance around, he asked, "So, you going to tell me what the deal is with you and Frances?"

It was a great question, but I didn't know how to explain why I'd lost my temper with Nick. Suddenly, I wondered if Frances knew about the fight. She must. I mean, everyone else seemed to. Was she mad? Happy? It shouldn't have mattered, but it did. "I don't know. Nothing, I guess."

"Come on, man, this is me you're talking to. You like her or something?"

"Or something," I muttered.

As if my thinking of her had the power to make her materialize, Frances set her tray down at a table in my line of sight.

"So, listen. Speaking of liking people, there's something I wanted to talk to you abo—"

"Hey, cool," I said, not really listening "Be right back."

Without giving myself a chance to think about it, I jumped out of my seat and headed over to Frances's table. Her friends saw me coming before she did, and they all looked up, eyes wide. For a panicked moment, I wondered if I had food on my face and wiped my hand over my mouth. "Hey," I said like a moron.

When Frances looked at me, her face turned red. *Uh-oh*, I thought. Was she angry after all?

"Hey," she replied.

Unsure what to say next, I looked back at Chris. He grinned and gave me two thumbs up. I cringed and turned away.

Stretching to the farthest reaches of my brain, I scraped for anything to say. "Uh, I finished the paper. Was wondering if you'd look at it."

She didn't say anything at first, and I started to worry she was going to tell me where I could stick my paper again, but finally she opened her mouth.

"Want to meet in the library after school?"

"Yeah, sure." I thought I saw the corner of her mouth twitch into a smile, so I smiled back. I had to meet the janitor after school, but no one gave me a specific time. Anyhow, what were they going to do if I was late? Kick me off the team?

"We missed you around here, Jesse," said Trevor. "Glad you're back."

I opened my mouth, but the girl sitting next to Frances jumped out of her seat and cut me off. "I'm Naomi." She grabbed my hand and shook it roughly. "It's so great to meet you."

"Uh, yeah, sure," I said, taking my arm back before she ripped it off. There was another girl, too. She hadn't looked interested when I first walked up, but now she cast a suspicious pair of eyes in my direction. "Hey," I said, a little unsure. "I'm Jesse."

The girl put down her iPad and crossed her arms. "Caterpillars are technically in the larval stage, so they don't mate."

"Sorry, what?"

"Sonny!" Frances frowned and flushed again. Obviously, I'd missed something because the girl shrugged, picked up her iPad, and resumed ignoring me.

"Don't mind Sonny," cut in Trevor. "She's pledged to speak in only astonishingly relevant insect code."

"Right..." I had no idea what he was talking about. "Well, I better get back to lunch. Good to see you, Trevor. Nice to meet you, Naomi...and Sonny." Everyone waved except Sonny, and I glanced at Frances who appeared to be looking at anyone but me. "See you later, Frances."

I noticed how she visibly cringed when I said her name, and I couldn't help but smile a little as I walked away.

I LEANED back on a library chair, precariously balanced on the two back legs. The library aide glared from her desk, but I pretended not to see her.

"Hi," said a voice behind me. I jumped, losing my fragile equilibrium and crashed to the floor in a stunning show of flailing arms.

"Oh, my gosh." Frances said and quickly pulled the chair off me. "Are you okay?"

I could feel the heat rise in my face. Smooth. *Real smooth.*

"Yeah, I'm fine." I snatched my backpack off the floor. I glanced over at the library aide and narrowed my eyes when I saw the smug look on her face.

"I didn't mean to scare you."

"Nah, you didn—I mean, don't worry about it."

We both sat, and an awkward silence fell over the table. Finally, I reached into my bag and handed her a red folder. "Here's the paper. It's probably terrible."

She took it from me and smiled. Frances didn't smile a lot, but when she did, it was a good one. It was the shy smile of someone who didn't think they were better than anyone else but kind of was.

I felt stupid sitting there while she read, so I shifted around in my chair and grabbed a pamphlet off the table. I think it was about volunteering, but I couldn't be sure because I only pretended to read it. After what felt like forever, she put the paper down and looked at me. I realized I was holding the pamphlet upside down and dropped it on the table.

"Jesse, this is really good." She sounded sincere, but I didn't miss the surprise in her voice.

"Nah," I said. "You mean, really good for a dumb person, right?"

She shook her head. "I mean really good for anyone, and you're not dumb."

"You're being nice."

She made an unintelligible sound and flipped through the paper. "I'm not that nice. The way you compared how all the husbands view their wives differently but then expect them to be equally subservient is fantastic."

"You think so? I thought it was kind of a stretch."

When she was excited about something, Frances's whole expression changed. It was like her voice was brighter. "It might be, but the way you write it is eloquent."

I didn't know what to say because I wasn't entirely sure what eloquent meant, but it sounded like a compliment. She leaned over to point out another line. She smelled like coconuts and the beach. We both realized at the same time how close we were, and she sucked in a breath and pulled away.

"I wanted to thank you," she said out of nowhere. "For standing up for me the way you did." She hesitated for a second, opening her mouth a few times before she continued. "And I'm sorry."

"Sorry for what?"

Instead of answering, she stared down at the table. I wished she would look at me so I'd have some chance at deciphering what she could be thinking. I reached over and touched the top of her hand. I don't know why I did it, other than it felt right in the moment. She jumped, and I yanked my hand back like I'd touched a burning stove.

"I should go." She stood up.

"Yeah? Oh, uh, okay." Feeling stupid, I stood up with her. She still wouldn't look at me, and I silently cursed. *Why the hell did I do that?*

She shot me a weak smile. "Yeah, so your paper is great, and you don't need my help anymore." Without another word, she bolted for the door.

I snatched my bag to try to keep up with her, but it caught on the back of the chair, and I struggled to get it loose. "Hey, wait up!" I called, but she either didn't hear me or pretended not to. When I looked up, all I saw were the library doors swinging closed.

THE ONLY GOOD thing about my indentured servitude was that it didn't start until everyone else had left, so no one would be around to see me scrubbing toilets or taking out trash. I rapped on the janitor's door, but when no one answered, I let it swing open. Inside, a pair of feet rested on top of a desk, the body attached hidden behind a stretched-out newspaper.

I poked my head in. "Hello?"

There was no response, so I stepped in. I must have cast a shadow because one corner of the newspaper lowered, and the janitor pulled an earbud out of one ear. "Jesse, right? Wasn't sure if you were going to show up."

"Yeah, sorry. I had to take care of some stuff." I didn't offer any further explanation, and he didn't ask for one.

"The one with all the girl trouble, right?" He offered me his hand, and I took it.

"I'm Bill," he added. "Don't look so down, kid. I haven't got much for you today. If you help me mop the cafeteria, we can call it a day. There is a game on tonight I don't want to miss."

I bowed. "I'm told I'm at your service."

Bill grinned. "Grab a mop."

It took a little over an hour to mop the cafeteria. You never grasp how disgusting high school kids are until you have to clean up after them. I made a mental note to make sure all my food made it into the trash can the next time lunch was over. There was a ring of dried rainbow splatter around every trash can. Much of it needed to be chiseled off with a butter knife. I wondered if scientists ever considered the potential of dried pizza sauce as an adhesive.

Bill didn't say much while we worked. He gave little direction and let me do my thing. I felt my body relax as the swoosh of the mop back and forth lulled me into a quiet trance. Before I knew it, Bill was leaning his mop up against the wall. "All done, kid."

I nodded and leaned my mop next to his. Outside, the setting sun cast a warm glow through the window. Bill followed my gaze, and we stood in silence for a few beats.

"Pretty, isn't it?" he said.

I shrugged. "It's just a sunset."

"Nothing wrong with noticing something beautiful," he said as we hauled our mops and buckets back to Bill's office.

CHAPTER 17

Jesse

I love to hear the crowd go crazy. During the electrified moments between plays, I would feel the excitement from the stands like an arcing current between me and the cheering people. That pulse doubled and tripled with every winning play. I never felt more alive than in those moments.

Sitting in the stands, on the other hand, was not so thrilling. I was small and anonymous, perched on the highest row. A few people recognized me and waved, but they walked away with a flicker of confusion on their faces. Although the video had finally been removed, pretty much everyone knew about my fight with Nick, but most did not know that I had been kicked off the team. I was surprised Mom let me go to the game, considering I was still grounded, but guilt over the divorce may have contributed to her diminished resolve. One of the few advantages of being a child of a newly broken home, I guess.

The game was painful to watch. Coach shouted commands from the sidelines, and seeing him from this new perspective made me wonder how he hadn't keeled over from a heart attack by now. The guys looked exhausted as Pine Ridge cut off every play. In the end, we were destroyed: 12-0. Even if the jerk part of me had wanted them to lose without me, all my glee evaporated as the new JV quarterback, Mike, got pounded into the turf. He threw so many incompletes that I lost count during the second half. There was nothing vindicating about hearing the crowd's cheers turn to disappointed sighs. A lot of people would blame Mike for the loss, but it wasn't his fault. He wasn't ready to be quarterback, and if I hadn't gotten myself kicked off, he wouldn't have had to try.

When the game ended, I made my way down the stands, ignoring the disenchanted grumbles around me. A few people acknowledged me, but I could feel their loaded looks on my back.

I noticed Sarah talking to one of the other cheerleaders on the sidelines. Before we broke up, she usually found me after the games, and a bunch of us would go out for food. Being her boyfriend came with friends and popularity that I hadn't missed until that moment. She didn't look unhappy though, even if the fog of defeat still hung thick in the air. If she saw me, she didn't let on.

On my way out, I bumped into Greg and Ryan. Both were part of our offense. Greg tended to have a short fuse, while Ryan followed him around like a puppy. They were covered in grass and looked pissed off. Seeing them made me wonder if coming here was a dumb idea. "Hey, guys," I said, unable to get away without being spotted.

Greg's look turned dark when he recognized me. "Well, if it isn't Jesse Harmon. Enjoy watching Mike blow the game for us?"

I didn't care about how badly they had lost, and I wasn't going to take crap from him. "I'm sure Mike did his best."

"That little shit couldn't throw a football to his mom ten feet away. But you're right; that probably was his best."

Ryan misread the tension and laughed out loud. We both looked at him until the noise died away.

"Well, see you guys around." I turned to go, but Greg was a sore loser, and I should have known he was looking for someone to blame.

"Yeah, you know, it was great of you to come down here and support the team like this," he threw sarcastically at my back.

I stopped and turned around. "If you have something to say, Greg, just say it."

Some of the other players stopped to watch. I spotted Mike off to the side, and I flinched at his swollen face. The rest of the team didn't look angry, but they weren't exactly happy to see me either.

Greg was a good two or three inches taller than me and stepped closer, making our height difference more noticeable. "I just think it sucks that one guy can throw an entire year away for the whole team."

"It was one scrimmage," I argued, not liking how close Greg's reasoning mirrored my own. "Anyway, I didn't throw anything. They kicked me off the team."

"Yeah," chimed in Ryan, unimpressed with my answer. "But what about next year?"

I glared at him but said nothing.

"Because Jesse does whatever he wants," Greg answered for me. "I just think if you were going to screw us over a girl, she'd at least be hot."

I closed the small gap between us so fast even he looked surprised. "What did you say?" My tone dared him to say it again.

Greg may have just been blowing off steam, but now he had been challenged, and I knew he wouldn't back down. We were close enough to trade swings, but Coach's arm suddenly shot between us.

"You want to go for expulsion, Harmon?" Coach asked, his voice as rough as sandpaper. "Because that's where you're headed." There was no way to know how much Coach had heard, but it was clear he wasn't going to take my side.

"Everyone goes home, *now*," he commanded.

Both Greg and I ignored him, but when Coach repeated Greg's name, it had a magical effect. Greg blinked, looked at him, and nodded before giving me one final glare as he stepped back. He stomped toward the locker room, Ryan nipping at his heels.

Coach shot me a withering glance. "Get out of here, Jesse. I don't want to see you at games if this is how it's going to be."

I opened my mouth to argue, but he turned his back on me and stalked to the field where a group of parents stood frowning at us.

The rest of the players ambled off, looking bored with the outcome. I'd noticed none of them had backed me up or even acknowledged me on their way out. So much for team solidarity.

I sighed when I noticed Mike still hanging back. He was hard to miss. The right side of his face looked so banged up that I wouldn't have been surprised if his eye was swollen shut by the time he got home. All I could say was, "I'm sorry, Mike."

He shrugged. "It's okay. Everyone gets beat up sometime, right?"

I was only a couple of years older, but he seemed like such a kid to me, and his optimism made me feel even worse. "You're going to want to put some ice on that when you get home."

Mike grinned a little. "Doesn't even hurt."

I found it hard to believe that Mike wasn't sore as hell, but after the beating he took in my place tonight, the least I could do was not call him out on it.

He pointed toward the parking lot. "My mom's waiting. Want a ride?"

"No, thanks," I said, needing some space. "I like walking."

He started to leave but stopped when I called out to him. "You did great tonight, Mike. Some nights are just like that."

"Wish you could come back, Jesse. It's not the same without you."

"Thanks," I muttered, but as I watched Mike jump into his mom's mini-van, I realized I'd done all this for a girl who probably didn't like me anyway. But knowing that still didn't make me regret it.

AFTER THE GAME, I settled down for a few hours of Netflix to take my mind off everything. After a couple of episodes of *Luke Cage*, I stepped out of the room for a drink. The light of the fridge illuminated the kitchen as I poured myself a glass of orange juice. Mom's voice drifted in from the bedroom, which was weird because she was usually asleep by now.

Mom used to volunteer at an art museum in the afternoons. She'd set up displays and teach art classes in the summer. When I was little, she'd take me with her. I remember sticking my hands in large jars of paint and smacking them against the cinderblock wall in the art room. When Mom caught me, she didn't even get mad. She stuck her own hands in the paint, and we covered all the walls with our prints. I hadn't been to the museum in a long time, but last time I was there, our handprints were still there.

When Dad left, she had to get a job as a secretary at a nursing home during the day, and the museum got a new art teacher to cover the summer. She never even talked about the museum anymore.

I closed the fridge door and stood in the dark, listening to her end of the conversation.

"What do you want me to do, Steve?" she said. "He's almost eighteen. We can't force him." There was a pause. "I do *not* undermine you. You're just going to have to accept that it's normal for him to be angry. Give him some time."

My hand tightened around the glass. They had it all figured out. Give him some time, and he'll forget that his dad's a liar, that he left us behind to start a *better* family.

There was another long silence before Mom spoke again. This time her voice was softer, more defeated. "I'll tell him, but please don't expect him to be cooperative."

Yeah, Steve, don't expect me to take your crap the way she does. I stomped off to my room and slammed the door, not caring if Mom heard. I flopped down on the bed, put my headphones on, and glared at the ceiling, willing myself to think of anything else. Somewhere between vowing never to get married and wishing my dad would get hit by a bus, I managed to fall asleep.

CHAPTER 18

Frances

"So, just to recap: he tried to hold your hand, so you ran away?" Trevor laughed so hard he almost choked on his hamburger. Thankfully, the roar of the Seminole Mall food court masked the sounds of my humiliation. We were waiting for Naomi, who was late as usual.

"I don't know why I told you," I said, scowling.

"You must really like him."

"No, I... He's..." I let out a long breath and tried to gather my thoughts into a complete sentence. "He just surprised me."

"Isn't it fantastic when that happens?" Trevor smiled, but I could only frown in return. He was enjoying this way too much.

Trevor whistled, reaching his arm over the top of the empty seat next to him. "Boy, you got it bad. Who would have thought you and the former football star, Jesse Harmon were soulmates?"

"Would you grow up? All I did was help him with his English paper, and now I can't hold my head up at school, thanks to you."

Trevor shrugged. "Don't exaggerate. Anyway, I was right, wasn't I? Jesse's little locker room cage match has boosted your social stock value."

"My what?"

"Face it. You're officially a commodity on the market."

"Great," I replied with a hefty dose of sarcasm. "And what if I liked being *off* the market?"

"You can't hide forever, Franny. Everyone gets dumped, humiliated, used, and treated like dirt. It's high school."

"Terrific," I said. "Thanks for the pep talk."

Trevor looked like he wanted to say more, but Naomi strolled up, swinging two large shopping bags. She dropped both bags on the table and fell into a chair. "What a day," she breathed.

"What is all that?" asked Trevor.

"These," she pointed to the bags, "are the two dresses I bought last week for prom. I couldn't decide which I liked better, the red chiffon or the sleek black, so I bought both to run through the normal battery of tests. I tried them with different shoes, hairstyles—you know."

"So, which one did you choose?" I asked.

"Neither."

"You bought two dresses for a date you don't even have yet?" Even Trevor looked stunned as we exchanged a look.

Naomi grinned, her features taking on a devilish appearance. "Oh, I have a date."

"You asked him?" Trevor asked, perking up.

"Nope."

"He asked you?" I ventured, but with serious doubts.

Naomi smiled. "Oh, he will."

"Oh, darling," Trevor cooed, "you've gone off the deep end. We need to call the authorities and have you hauled away before you do any more damage."

Naomi rolled her eyes. "You'll see. So, are you guys ready to go shopping?"

Trevor's phone vibrated, and he snatched it off the table as if worried we'd beat him to it. After some quick thumb work, he said, "Actually, I just remembered I need to finish that history paper I was working on. It's due soon." He jumped out of his seat, looking distracted. "I'll catch up with you ladies later."

"But I thought you finished that paper last week," called Naomi as he disappeared into a crowd of shoppers.

I raised an eyebrow. "Did he just lie to us?"

"I think so," replied Naomi, sounding pensive. "I wonder what's up with him?"

It wasn't like Trevor to hide things, but I was nothing if not understanding of a person's need for privacy. "I'm sure it's fine. You ready to head out?"

We walked the length of two stores in Naomi's epic search for the perfect prom dress, but after three hours I was ready to go home. Macy's was quiet except for the occasional ring of a nearby cell phone or passing shopper. I scanned through a rack of dresses I had no hope of fitting into while Naomi tried on another array of possible choices.

My hand slid several gowns across the rack, but I wasn't really looking at them. It wasn't like I really *wanted* to go to prom. I just needed to get the crown, toss Lena a smug look, and walk out, right? There was no one going that I wanted to see, other than Naomi and her new fake boyfriend. Yet, a thought I barely allowed myself to acknowledge buzzed along the edges of my mind like an invisible mosquito. *What if Jesse asked me?*

I squashed the idea before it had a chance to draw blood. *Why would Jesse want to go with me after all the trouble I caused him?*

Sensing someone behind me, I turned and froze when I saw Jesse's girlfriend—or ex-girlfriend— also looking at dresses. I couldn't believe my bad luck. She had her back to me and raised two dresses in front of her, appraising each. One was a soft pink, a little off the shoulder, and the other a knee-length red dress that looked too mature for her. I didn't think she'd seen me yet, so I figured that if I were quiet, I might be able to get to the dressing room, grab Naomi, and sneak out before she noticed me. But of course, as I took my first retreating step back, I tripped and fell into the rack of clothes, almost toppling it over.

At first, Sarah looked startled, and I thought maybe she didn't recognize me. But her bright ice-blue eyes flashed and narrowed. *Oh, she recognized me all right.*

My smile was grim as I tried to rebalance myself, straightening the disheveled clothes along the rack. Maybe this didn't have to be so terrible. "I like the pink one," I said, trying my best to sound friendly, but she glared at me before slamming the pink dress back on the rack and stalking away.

I sighed, my eyes lifting to the ceiling. *Where was a big dark hole when a girl needed one?* I fled to the dressing room to find Naomi, so we could get the hell out of there.

———

THAT NIGHT, I listened to the rain hit the roof as I washed the last of the dinner dishes. It was getting late, and Dad had wandered off to bed an hour ago.

Mom was out with her sponsor, Gina. If she had a tough day or felt stressed, Gina would always come to the rescue. In the beginning, I was relieved Gina was there. She had a way of keeping Mom on track, and her depressive moods didn't seem so bad when Gina was there to help. But the more time they spent together, the more annoyed I became with her presence. Why did Mom deserve all that constant attention? When she came home from rehab, I thought things would get better, but I quickly learned that anything I needed would always take a backseat to Mom's recovery.

I cringed when the front door opened and I heard the sound of Mom's umbrella hitting the bucket in the hall. I finished the last dish and rolled my eyes. She was right on time, in the door the moment all the work was done.

"Hey, sweetheart. How are you?" she asked as I put a container of spaghetti in the fridge.

"Fine," I said dryly. "Leftovers are in the fridge." I started to move past her, but she reached out a hand and stopped me.

"Hey, sit down a minute. There's something I want to talk to you about."

I stared at her but allowed her to guide me into a kitchen chair. "Okay."

She sat down too, wiping brown hair away from her bright brown eyes. Dad always said we had the same eyes, but I could never see it.

"Lately, you and I haven't had much time together, have we?"

I didn't respond, hoping she would get to the point.

"There's this camp," she continued, pulling a brochure from her bag. "It's just outside Seminole County, and it has lots of great cabins, horseback riding, and hiking. You always loved all that nature stuff."

I imagined Dad was behind this sudden interest in quality time, but she was right. I did love camping. We used to go all the time when I was a kid, but that seemed like a lifetime ago. "And you want to go?" I asked, a little dazed.

"Of course." Her voice was so musical. I couldn't stop my lips from twitching into a half smile. "It's next weekend, and we could go on Friday," she sing-songed. "We'll make it a long weekend."

Starstruck by the idea, I picked up the brochure. "Would Dad come?"

She smiled and touched my hand. "I think Dad could sit this one out. I'd like it to be just the two of us...if you don't mind?"

I couldn't believe what I was hearing. She was going to drop everything—the AA meetings, the fundraisers, the sponsors—just to go camping with me? With the pamphlet open on the table, I poured over the first page. Once I got to the inside, the bottom fell out of my stomach. "This is an AA event."

She nodded with enthusiasm. "Oh yes, our group leader booked the weekend for us. We get to do all the camping stuff you like, plus I can still attend AA meetings. I told Gina I would volunteer to run a couple of the welcome meetings, but they'll only tie me up for the first half of the day. After that, I'm all yours."

I stared at the brochure, feeling my face burn with fury. I was so *stupid*. I should have known this was all about her. "I can't go." I struggled to keep my voice even. "I have an exam on Monday to study for."

Her smile fell away. "Are you sure? Can't you do a makeup test or something, or study when you get home?"

"It's a midterm," I lied. "If I don't do well, it could mess up my grades for the whole semester." I got up, leaving the brochure on the table.

Mom frowned. "If you say so...but will you at least think about it? I mean, maybe you could study while you're there. I could help you."

She looked so disappointed that I almost wavered. Maybe a part of her did want to spend time with me, but I just couldn't stomach being around all her AA buddies for an entire weekend, listening to them congratulate each other for being so brave and resilient while I sat in the corner waiting for Mom to notice me. "Maybe some other time, but you should still go. I'm sure you'll have a blast."

Mom looked down at the brochure. "Well, I guess I could. I was looking forward to running those sessions, and Gina's going to be there with her daughter, Tammy."

"Well," I said, squaring my shoulders, "don't let me hold you back."

I left her in the kitchen to pour over the brochure and make plans. As I headed upstairs, I reminded myself that I didn't care what she did, even as I wiped away the angry tears spilling down my cheeks.

CHAPTER 19

Jesse

"Where do you think you're going?" called Mom from the kitchen as I headed for the front door. "You're still grounded."

I stopped, my hand still on the doorknob. Other than the game, I'd been on house arrest for almost two weeks. "Mom, come on. I did everything you asked me to do, *and* I wrote my English paper. I'm doing community service, and I'm off the football team. Haven't I suffered enough?"

Her face relaxed a little. Pity. Fine. I'd take what I could get.

"Well," she started, looking a little guilty. "The thing is..."

That didn't sound good. "What?"

"Your dad's coming over later. He wants to take you to Bellini's." She cringed a little. It must have been the look on my face.

"No way."

She sighed and pressed the base of her palm to her forehead. "Jesse, please. It's time. Your father wants to talk to you. As much as I hate to force the issue, we can't put this off any longer."

"He wants to go to Bellini's?"

"You love Bellini's."

I used to love it. Our family wasn't Italian, but Dad always liked to pretend we were. We'd stop there on our way through DeLand and order two giant plates of chicken alfredo in the middle of the day. Then we'd roll into the house, stuffed but satisfied. It used to be amazing, just like our family. "You're doing it again. Stop pretending everyth—"

"Jesse. I don't want to argue. Your father will be here at six to pick you up, and you need to be prepared to go."

She was playing the heavy; she'd done it when Dad was around. Mom was quick to punish, but Dad was always willing to hear me out. He played good cop to her bad, but Dad was gone, and the old routine didn't work anymore. "Can I go now?"

"*Only* if you promise to be back by six." She pulled my phone out of her purse. "Here, take this just in case."

I stared longingly at the phone in her hand. *Damn her.* Did she think she could bribe me into having dinner with Dad by offering me my phone back? She did, and she could.

I took the phone and held the power button down until I heard the beautiful tones of the startup.

"I mean it, Jesse. In the door by six. You promise?"

I was already out the door when I called back over my shoulder, "Got it. Six!" I'd almost said that if she hoped for a nice father-son chat tonight, she shouldn't hold her breath. But decided I wanted the phone more than I wanted to make a point.

CHAPTER 20

Frances

"So, I texted Webb and told him I needed to ask him a few more questions for the article. He's meeting me at Boston Coffee House after school on Monday."

"Naomi, I think you're taking this too far." Actually, I was sure she was, but I hoped she'd see it for herself. We were waiting for Trevor outside the movie theater just inside the mall. We'd already bought the tickets, and if he didn't show up soon, we were going to miss the previews.

"Am not," she argued. "I'm building a base for our relationship. It's all pa—"

"Part of the plan. Right," I said, cutting her off. "But have you considered how much this master plan of yours just sounds like a lot of lying? I mean, you're practically dating this guy, and he doesn't even know it."

Naomi gave me a look that said I wasn't seeing the bigger picture. "It's not lying, Franny. It's..." she looked up, searching for the right words. "...romantic."

I didn't argue but hoped for her sake that Webb shared Naomi's warped sense of romance. I checked my phone again. "You told him five, right?"

Naomi shrugged. "Yeah, but I'll text him." A few minutes later, she got a text back. "He says he's not coming," Naomi said with a frown.

"Since when?"

"I don't know." Her brow creased with worry. "He just said something came up. Franny, do you think something's wrong?"

"If something were wrong, he would have said so."

"He's been so secretive lately." Naomi stuffed her phone into her pocket and fidgeted with her hands. She and Trevor were close. I doubted there was much going on in either of their lives the other didn't know about. "Do you think he's on drugs or something?" asked Naomi.

"Whoa, how did we go from him flaking out on a movie to drugs? Naomi, are we going in or—"

The sound of my startled shriek echoed off the high ceilings, and I smacked my hand over my mouth as if that could take back the spectacle. Jesse Harmon stood right beside me.

"Sorry," he said, but his lips curved into a crooked smile. "Didn't mean to scare you."

"What are you doing here?" was all I could croak out as I stared, stunned by his sudden presence.

"Hanging out. I mean, I was just leaving when I saw you guys." He looked a little unsure. "I thought I'd say hi." He wore a pair of faded jeans and a plain blue t-shirt under a flannel. It was a simple outfit that looked like it required only the bare minimum of effort, yet, somehow, he still looked amazing in it.

Naomi, who had been uncharacteristically silent up till then, tried to save the conversation, but the ship was sinking fast. "Well, we're glad you did. Aren't we, Franny?"

When I didn't respond, Naomi nudged me, but all I could do was nod my head. Apparently, I'd lost all communication and most of my motor skills.

Naomi cast me an exasperated look. "We were going to go see the new *Spiderman*. Do you want to come with us? Look, we have an extra ticket!" Naomi snatched Trevor's ticket from my hand and offered it to Jesse.

Motor function returned long enough for my eyes to bug out of my head. *What the heck did she think she was doing?*

"Well...uh," he started, and glanced at his cell phone.

I scowled at Naomi, stuck between cursing the ground she stood on and waiting to see what Jesse would say.

"Actually," said Naomi, "I just remembered Mom wanted me home tonight because, uh, it's...family night."

I gaped at her. "I'm sorry... Did you say *family night?*" Naomi's family could barely manage a single meal together, let alone the quality time needed for a successful "family night."

"Yeah, you know." She gave me a meaningful look. "We always have family night. Board games, and other, uh...family things. Anyway, you guys should go. Have a great time!" Before I knew what was happening, Naomi was speed walking away from us, leaving zero time for me to threaten her or renounce our friendship.

Jesse looked just as dumbfounded at Naomi's sudden departure as I was. My throat was dry when I spoke. "You don't have to go if you don't want to."

He looked at me. His face was unreadable except for that crooked smile, which was somehow both endearing and obnoxious. "What time does it start?"

I looked at my phone. "In a few minutes."

He glanced at his phone one more time before he turned it off and slid it in his pocket. "We'd better get going. I hate missing the previews."

THE MOVIE WAS GOOD, but when it was over, I couldn't recall any of the major plot points. I was too distracted sitting in the theater with Jesse. Once, his arm brushed mine, and I jumped in my seat like he'd stung me. I felt foolish for the overreaction.

When the movie was over, neither one of us said anything as we walked out. Jesse turned his phone back on and frowned.

"Everything okay?" I asked.

"Nothing important."

My stomach felt hollow. Maybe I was trying to be brave, but I let the words flow out of me before I gave myself an opportunity to change my mind. "There's a pizza place next door. Want to get something to eat?"

He looked distracted again, but before I could overthink it, he typed out a text and slipped his phone back in his pocket. "Sounds good. Let's go."

Pizza City was a family restaurant my parents used to take me to when I was younger, although we hadn't been in years. My breath came up short when the waitress showed us to an intimate table in a dimly lit corner of the restaurant. It had a red and white checkered tablecloth with a candle melted over an empty wine bottle in the center. I hadn't remembered the restaurant as having such a romantic setting, and I could feel the blood rush to my face.

"Cool place," he remarked as we sat down.

"Yeah," I said. "It's uh...changed a lot since the last time I was here."

He looked at the menu. "Want to split a pizza?"

I nodded and tried to swallow the golf ball-sized lump in my throat. All I could think of was how ridiculous this was and how there was no way he really wanted to be here. The back of my neck turned hot, and I wiped a palm full of sweat from my forehead.

"Pepperoni and extra cheese?"

Again, I nodded. What was wrong with me? Why couldn't I speak? I tried to slow my breathing, but my heart pounded in my ears and all the air seemed to leave the room. Overwhelmed by the sudden pressure on my lungs, the restaurant rolled to the side, and I had to grip the table for support.

I closed my eyes and heard Jesse ask if I was okay, but his voice sounded far away. I tried to nod, but I had to cover my face with my other hand to shield myself from the spinning room. Someone else walked up to the table, but I didn't catch what Jesse said to them. Then they were gone, and Jesse was crouched next to my chair, his large hand gripping mine. His voice sounded anxious, but

I was too focused on trying not to vomit all over him to reassure him.

"Frances, are you okay? Talk to me."

The waitress returned with a glass of ice water. Jesse took it from her and put my hands around the glass. The icy condensation felt good on my hot skin. "Here, drink this," he instructed, and I downed several large gulps as the world gradually settled back on its axis.

The waitress looked worried. "Is there anything else I can get you? Should I call an ambulance?"

I shook my head. "No, I think I'm good now," I said, even though I was anything but good. My hands were shaking, and I wanted to curl into a ball and disappear.

She nodded and told us she would be back in a few to take our order.

"Thanks for the water," I whispered.

Jesse hesitated but returned to his seat. "No problem," he said. "Do you want more?"

It was a simple question, but I didn't know how to answer. "I get panic attacks sometimes," I blurted, feeling my face flush anew. "But I'm fine now."

I closed my eyes again, ignoring how crazy I must look. "If you want to go, it's okay. I'll be fine now."

There was a long pause before either of us said anything, and I kept my eyes closed, afraid to see the look on his face. Just when I was sure he must have walked out, Jesse said, "Are you kidding? I'm starving. I'm not going anywhere until I've had some pizza."

I opened my eyes to find him smiling at me, and some of the tension drained from my shoulders. "Me too," I agreed, allowing my features to transform into a smile, "but I don't think we are going to see that waitress for a while."

He chuckled. "You really know how to make things interesting, don't you?" His phone chimed and he pulled it out of his pocket, and I was grateful to have the attention off me. He glanced at it before shoving it into his pocket again.

"So, what's that all about?" I asked.

"I was supposed to meet someone tonight," he shrugged. "It's no big deal."

That explained why he kept checking his phone. "I didn't mean to mess up your plans."

"You didn't," he said. "I'd rather be here with you."

An awkward silence fell over the table as we both digested what he'd just admitted. He didn't say anything more, but even in the dimly lit room I could see bits of red highlight his cheeks.

The waitress returned and took our order. She looked uncomfortable, and I tried to hide my exasperation as she eyed me warily.

Jesse must have noticed, too, because as soon as she left, he leaned forward and asked, "Should I pretend to have a seizure when she comes back?"

I laughed, and so did he, and it took a moment to get ourselves under control. "There's an idea, but we probably shouldn't. I think she's had all the excitement she can take for one day."

Jesse grinned. "Too bad. Bet I could make her change careers."

My anxious feelings melted away when I realized we were actually having a good time.

As if he could read my thoughts, Jesse said, "You know, you're not as crazy as everyone thinks you are."

I took another sip of my water. "I'll assume you meant that as a compliment."

"I did," he said, "but there is something I've been wanting to ask you."

"Okay." But I couldn't imagine what it might be.

"I don't understand why you want to be prom queen."

"That's not a question," I pointed out, feeling like someone just pulled the drain on our good time. "Anyway, who says I do?"

He gave me an odd look, as if he were trying to solve a puzzle. "You try pretty hard to fool people into thinking you don't care."

"But not you, right?" I'd meant it sarcastically, but instead of giving me a cheap comeback, his slow, lopsided grin made my heart stop. Honestly, I'd never known anyone who had such a beautiful yet punchable face.

I didn't feel right about relaying all the gory details of Sonny's run-in with Lena, so I tried to think of a witty explanation. The problem with that was my usual cynicism seemed out of place with Jesse. "What about you? Weren't you nominated for king?"

He shrugged. "It doesn't matter. Anyway, I'm pretty sure it was Sarah that nominated me."

The question of why Jesse and Sarah broke up screamed inside of me, but I knew better than to ask. This led to another uncomfortable silence. *Where was an emergency subject change when a girl needed one?* Fortunately, our waitress showed up with our pizza, and Jesse focused all his attention on devouring his food. It was amazing how easily distracted boys could be.

The pizza smelled spicy and familiar, and we both ate several pieces while Jesse told me all about Chris's obsession with *World of Warcraft* and his genius little sister.

In return, I talked about Trevor and Naomi, and about how we'd somehow absorbed Sonny into the group.

"That's pretty cool," he said. "I've never known anyone who spoke caterpillar before."

I smiled. "Sonny usually manages to get her point across." Without understanding why, I was relieved Jesse seemed okay with Sonny.

After a while, I looked around and realized that the restaurant was almost empty and the staff was starting to clean up. "We'd better go," I said. "It's getting late." My voice sounded more disappointed than I'd meant it to.

We split the check and walked to my car. "Can I give you a lift home?"

He nodded and looked at his phone again with a sigh. "Yeah, thanks, I'm pretty sure I missed the last bus."

Jesse didn't say much on the way except to give me directions.

Our jovial mood in the restaurant faded, and I tried my best not to speculate on what he was thinking. When we pulled into his driveway, I realized that Jesse only lived a mile or so from my house.

I put the car into park, and Jesse looked at me. "I had a good time."

I wanted to say I did, too, and that I didn't want it to end, but I couldn't figure out a way to say it without sounding like an idiot. So instead, I forced a smile and nodded.

His eyes felt like bright flashlights in the dark. "Maybe," he said, sounding less assured, "we could do it again sometime."

Say something, Frances! Where was a voice box when a girl needed one? When I was finally able to mold sound into words, I replied, "Sure, maybe," but winced at how guarded it sounded.

The moment passed and Jesse thanked me for the ride and got out of the car. He walked up the drive without looking back, even though I wished he would.

CHAPTER 21

Jesse

Mom cast me a murderous glare when I walked through the door.

"Hey," I said, bracing for impact.

She took a couple of deep breaths and stared at me. It didn't look like she'd been crying, at least not in the last few minutes. Maybe she was trying to keep her cool. Either way, I didn't think I should interrupt her.

"Do you know what I've been through tonight because of you?"

I sighed and sat down at the table with her. I hated making Mom's life harder, so for that part, I was sorry. "I sent you a text so you wouldn't worry."

"Yes, Jesse. Thank you for your illuminating 'out with friends' text message," she said, making quote marks in the air. "That really cleared things up for me." Her tone was dripping with raw anger. "We had a deal. Your father and I were worried about you."

"You shouldn't have tried to force me to see him." I knew I was pushing my luck, but I also knew I was right.

She looked down again and took my hand in hers. She squeezed it so tight I almost pulled away. "Jesse, I am fighting hard to make this divorce simple for both of us, but when you do things like get into fights and don't tell us where you are, it makes everything worse. Your father waited here for you most of the night. Do you have any idea what that was like for me?"

I frowned, thinking of him in the house again. How long had it been since the day he told me about the baby and the divorce all in the same breath? Six months? Longer? "If he's so worried, where is he now?"

"He had to go home." Her tone was dry with a bitter edge. "Kim wasn't feeling well."

I snorted. "Of course. He had to go home to his new family."

"Is that why you did this?" she asked. "To see if he would look for you?"

"I don't care what he does," I said bitterly.

"Jesse, no matter what he's done, your father lov—"

I snatched my hand away and stood up so fast the chair almost toppled over. "So, am I grounded again or what?"

I hated how sad her eyes looked. For a second, I considered agreeing to see him just to make things easier for her. But why couldn't she understand? Giving in was like saying I was okay with what he'd done, and that was something I could never do.

"Another week," she said, her voice tight. "Next time I tell you to be home and you don't show up, it'll be a month."

I walked to my room. What more was there to say? My mind went back to the restaurant. When Frances panicked, there was this moment while I was holding her hand where my parents, school, the team, everything faded away and I'd actually felt normal again. I ran over that moment again and again until I fell asleep.

CHAPTER 22

Frances

"Which of the following is an example of a symbiotic relationship?" I tried and failed to keep the annoyance out of my voice. The class was divided into pairs, tasked to answer the questions at the end of our biology chapter, but thanks to Naomi, we hadn't gotten very far.

"Do you think Webb is a good dancer?"

Lately all conversations orbited around Webb. His favorite food or what music he listened to—it was classic rock mixed with a little nineties alternative and new age. I shouldn't have known that, but I did. I was getting sick of Webb, and I didn't even know the guy. "Can we focus, please?"

"Huh? Oh, uh, a wolf pack?"

"Did you actually look that up?" I picked up the book and flipped through the pages.

Naomi sighed and smiled, leaning her head in her palm. "Who can think about biology at a time like this?"

"A time like what?" I asked as I skimmed the section titles for the answer.

"When we are both in love."

I glowered at her over the top of the book. "I'm not in love, and neither are you. The answers are due by the end of class."

Naomi ignored me. "So, Jesse wants to eat lunch with you today?"

I tried to focus on what I was reading, but she was making it hard.

"This morning when I saw him, he mentioned he and Chris might sit at our table."

"Aren't you excited?"

"Because he said he *might* eat lunch at our table?"

"*Noooo*, because he asked if he could eat lunch with *you*," she said with a silly smile that implied way more than was reasonable.

"You're making a big deal out of nothing. Just promise me you're not going to be how you get."

She reached over and pulled the book out of my hands. "And how do I get?"

"*You know*," I said and took the book back.

She laughed. "I really don't. Tell me."

"This." I drew imaginary circles around her face. "Over-excited. You overwhelm people."

Her jaw dropped. "When have I ever done that?"

I opened my mouth to say something, but Mrs. McGee gave us a five-minute warning, and I refused to discuss anything more until our work was done.

We managed to find most of the answers by the end of class. We turned the sheet in with both our names on it, even though Naomi's only contribution was putting the book away on our way out the door.

With Naomi still chattering away, we entered the cafeteria, and the familiar creep of anxiety worked its way into my shoulders. I took several deep breaths as we picked up our trays and made our way through the lunch line. I tried to glance around without making it seem like I was looking, but that's about as effective as it sounds. I barely registered that the lunch lady had dropped a scoop of chicken salad on my plate. By the time we got to the table, I was a wreck.

Trevor and Sonny were already at the table, their heads together as Sonny showed Trevor something on her iPad. They were both smiling, but as we walked up, Trevor drew the iPad down and put a finger to his lips. Sonny mimicked the gesture.

"What are you two up to?" I asked.

"That's between me and the caterpillar," replied Trevor with an air of superiority.

I looked at Sonny, but she just smiled and put her finger over her lips again.

I was annoyed, but since Trevor didn't mention Jesse or our visit to the movies—even though I was sure Naomi told him—I let it go. Naomi and Trevor chatted about some reality show that had caught their interest as I casually looked around the cafeteria. My shoulders dropped in disappointment. No Jesse. Maybe he changed his mind.

On one of my scans of the room, my gaze paused on Nick Temple. I hadn't realized how absent he'd been. He *was* sitting with his friends, but...he wasn't talking or laughing in the obnoxious way he always did. He just sat there, hunched over his tray a few seats apart from everyone else.

"Hey." Jesse and Chris walked up, and all thoughts of Nick evaporated.

"Hey," I said like an idiot.

They both sat, and I smiled at Chris. "How's it going?"

The look of surprise on Chris's face made me want to laugh. His eyes widened, and he looked to Jesse, as if asking for help. Had I really been that mean to him?

"Uh...not bad...Frances," Chris replied. "You?"

I pretended he hadn't called me Frances. My feelings on the subject didn't seem to matter lately, anyway. "Good, thanks."

Naomi looked like she was about to explode into a million enthusiastic pieces, so I sighed and introduced everyone to Chris.

Naomi smiled her most dazzling smile. "Charmed, I'm sure."

Sonny gave Chris a thumbs up, but otherwise ignored him.

Trevor leaned back in his chair and grinned. "We've met."

I gave them both a questioning look. "You have?"

"We have gym together," Trevor reminded me, and my face flushed at the recollection of what happened there.

"Right. I forgot," I muttered.

"So," Trevor said, breaking the awkward silence that settled over the table. "Anyone heard any decent Marvel spoilers lately?"

Conversation flowed smoothly from there. I'd never been more grateful for Trevor's and Naomi's endless supply of chatty energy. We talked about movies, which moved the conversation to comic books, which seemed to spark Chris's attention. Jesse and I stayed mostly quiet, interjecting only occasionally when there were pauses in the conversation, which wasn't often.

I was astonished by how everyone seemed to get along. I'd always thought of Trevor, Naomi, and myself as outcasts, of Jesse and his friends as social leaders, but there was no evidence of this grand class division now. Even Sonny, who stayed silent most of the time, would take a position on the occasional debate by offering a thumbs up. This always ended with the winning side going, "See! Even Sonny knows I'm right."

In the middle of a bout of laughter, I glanced at Jesse and caught him looking at me. His eyes darted away, but after a moment they rose again, shy but curious, and we both smiled. It was a frightening and exhilarating few seconds, like we both had a secret to share. I cursed the bell when it rang and broke the magic spell.

CHAPTER 23

Sonny

Dale always smelled like markers. His backpack was covered in colorful spots around the pocket edges where capless Sharpies bled into the fabric. He scribbled into a sketch book. I strained my neck to see, but the movement caught his eye, and he covered the drawing with his elbow.

I sighed and pulled out my iPad. Mr. Hernandez was absent, and I glared at the substitute who sat at the desk, her eyes focused on her phone rather than on us. She said we could have a free period, but I missed the way our *real* teacher never sat at the desk at all.

I frowned when a low battery notification popped up in the middle of my iPad screen. School was almost over, but losing battery was never an option. I glanced around for a place to plug in my charger, but they were all taken up by classroom equipment. Everyone else was talking, and their loud voices grated against my temples like buzzing bees. I bit my lip and tapped the top of my head, hoping somehow it would drown out the sound of their terrible chatter.

My eyes shot open when a hand caught mine. Fingertips stained with color gingerly touched my wrist between long, thin fingers. I stopped tapping and looked at Dale, who took his hand away and motioned for the iPad.

I hesitated, but his serious expression told me he understood how important it was, so I handed it over. He took it carefully and plugged it in to a white cord attached to a mobile power bank. The iPad began to charge and the knot in my stomach uncurled. Before he handed it back, he inspected the picture on my home screen.

It was one of my drawings. The outline of a butterfly. Trevor really liked it, but it wasn't finished yet. Dale tapped a few things on the iPad before handing it back to me. He appeared to wrestle with something before he lifted his own drawing pad off the table to reveal his artwork. It was a glorious beast, a dragon full of reds and blues, all colored in Sharpie but blended so you couldn't tell when one color ended and another began. The creature spat flames that were too hot to touch as it burned away the paper to reveal the drawing on the next page: a knight brandishing a sword.

He lowered his notepad, and I was stunned to realize that all of his scribbling was more like magic. I looked around the classroom, wondering if anyone noticed our exchange, but Rocky and Gigi were still giggling and talking.

A notification on my iPad drew my attention. A message from an unknown person read: *What program did you use to add the wings?*

I looked up and Dale was staring at me meaningfully, his cell phone in hand.

Clutching the iPad, I typed out my answer: *Photoshop.*

Dale's phone chimed, and his fingers slid across the screen. *Why did you make it?*

I bit my lower lip but quickly typed my response, hoping the bell didn't ring before I had a chance to tell him. *Can you keep a secret?*

CHAPTER 24

Frances

First, it was a couple of girls standing by the school entrance. Their conversation abruptly ended as I approached, and their eyes, donned in glitter eyeshadow, followed me with keen interest as I walked past. I glanced back at them but kept going, trying not to assume that their sudden silence had anything to do with me.

Next, it was a slap on the back by some guy I didn't know. He was tall and had a skateboard in one hand. With the other, he smacked my back with enough force to make me stumble forward. "Nice," he said and kept moving down the hall.

I stared after him. "Ooo-kay." The looks and smiles continued all the way down the hall. Mike, whom I recognized from the football team, grinned at me as he passed. He was sporting a nasty shiner, and I wondered what the other guy looked like. "Cool flyer, Franny," he said.

I stared after him. "What flyer?" But apparently he didn't hear me over the noise of the hallway, and I was left to wonder if he had me confused with someone else.

When I reached the first cross-section of the main hallway, I stopped short, unable to fully take in what I was looking at.

Plastered on every locker and door were bright rainbow flyers. Each one had a picture of me flanked by a pair of technicolor butterfly wings that stretched out across the page. In the picture, my eyes were closed in serene meditation. The color of the wings bled into the paper like running ink. On top of the flyer, "Frances" was scrawled in elegant lettering, and on the bottom in bold block letters: "IS QUEEN".

Oh. My. Hell.

A few things ran through my mind as I stared at what seemed like a thousand copies of...me. First, I wondered when that picture was taken. Second, I tried to estimate how long it would take to rip them all down, and how crazy I would look doing it. I didn't get an opportunity to consider either for very long because Trevor slammed into me, trailing Naomi and Sonny behind him.

"Isn't it fantastic?" The three of them wore such bright, excited expressions, that I couldn't even speak. A dull moan was all I could manage.

"Everyone is talking about it," gushed Naomi. "They are so crazy beautiful. People are putting them up in their lockers and using them as book covers!"

I stared at them, hoping someone would fill me in on how this could have happened.

"Now, I know you're too grateful for words," Trevor said, "but I can't take all the credit. The artwork is all Sonny."

My gaze shifted to Sonny, who nudged Trevor and gave him a meaningful look.

"Oh, and her friend Dale helped with distributing," he amended.

Sonny smiled, and a sudden wave of nausea swept over me. Did they truly not see how insane this was? How crazy, impractical, how... but when I looked into Sonny's radiant face, all my horror melted away. She was so proud of herself that she gave off a faint glow. Something about this recognition gave her a presence I'd never seen before. It made me think about the girl hiding behind the water fountain, and I sighed.

"I love it." I stretched my hand in the air to give her a thumbs up. "Thank you, Sonny." Although the words felt dry in my mouth.

Sonny beamed and raised her own thumb into the air, followed by Trevor and Naomi.

"Well, hello, Team Frances," sang Theo, the editor of the student newspaper. He strolled up with a clip board under one arm and slid the other around Trevor's shoulders. Theo was tall and always wore the latest styles a week before anyone else, which made sense because he wrote a style column for the paper. "How are we all doing this morning, campaigners?"

"Terrific," said Trevor. "As you can see, our little ad campaign is a big hit, and it's getting a ton of response on social media, especially Instagram."

"It's on Instagram?" I choked out.

Trevor ignored me. "What's the word, Theo? You got good news for me?"

My gaze darted back and forth between them. "What are you talking about?"

Theo flashed me a wide smile. "I just left an emergency meeting with the newspaper staff, and it's decided. The student newspaper will officially be endorsing Frances for prom queen." Theo made this statement with an air of superiority that implied this vital endorsement would all but clinch the crown for me.

Trevor and Theo fist-bumped while Naomi actually jumped up and down in place, waving her arms with excitement. Sonny and I were the only two unmoved by the news. "I don't understand," I said. "Since when does the student newspaper do endorsements?"

"Since now," Theo replied. "Frances, this is no ordinary competition. People love an underdog. The morning poll has you neck and neck with Lena, and we still have a few weeks to go."

My mouth fell open. "You're polling people?"

Theo shrugged. "Just a few hundred kids."

Trevor grabbed my arm as I reached for Theo, rapidly considering all the places I could cram that clipboard.

"That's awesome news," said Trevor hastily. "I better get her to class before she's late. We don't want anyone saying our new queen isn't a committed student."

I allowed Trevor to steer me away from sudden bloodshed, but I imagined huge plumes of smoke billowing from my ears. Had the whole school gone crazy? I waited until we were out of earshot before whirling on Trevor. "This has gone too far."

"Franny, *this* is what it takes to win."

"*This*," I motioned at the flyers strewn all over the hallway, "is insanity. I am not a side-show act."

"May I remind you, Your Majesty, that you *asked* me to help you become queen. Do you think all this was easy? I had to run to an all-night printer *and* call in a lot of favors to get these posters put out this morning. The least you could do is play the part."

"But I don't want to play any part. I jus—"

"Franny, this isn't about you anymore. Did you see Sonny's face? If you don't see this through, you're going to break her heart and disappoint a lot of people who want to see the little guy win for a change." He looked down the edge of his aristocratic nose at me. "So, stop whining and start acting like the queen everyone needs you to be."

I stared at him, the weight of his words falling heavily on my shoulders. He was right about one thing: I'd asked for all of it, and it was too late to back out now.

CHAPTER 25

Jesse

In English, we'd moved on from *The Taming of the Shrew* to *Romeo and Juliet*. Ms. Blackwell called on one of the kids in the back to read, and I tried to keep my head propped up with my palm so I wouldn't fall asleep, but it was a struggle. It's not like we didn't all know the story.

"Why, then, O brawling love," read the student, "O loving hate, O anything of nothing first create, O heavy lightness, serious vanity, Misshapen chaos of well-seeming forms, Feather of lead, bright smoke, cold fire, sick health, Still-waking sleep that is not what it is. This love feel I, that feel no love in this."

I wished *I* could find some waking sleep. My heavy eyes focused on the clock. I needed to meet Bill after school. Picking up trash had to be less boring than this.

A packet of paper dropped in front of me, and I shot up like someone fired a gun at my desk. Blackwell raised a thin brow, and my sheepish smile was all the proof she needed that I wasn't paying attention. I turned the paper over. It was *the* paper. It was covered in red ink. Apparently, there had been quite a few grammatical errors, sentence restructures, and misused words, but at the top was a giant letter A circled with a smiley face and the note: *Love your angle!*

I looked at Blackwell, who met my gaze with an approving smile.

"Look, there's another one. These damn flyers are everywhere." Bill snatched the colorful paper off the grass and started to crumple it up. We'd worked our way around the football field with long sticks and old paint buckets to collect trash.

"Hang on." I took it from him. I smoothed out the edges against my jeans before rolling it up and sticking it in my pocket.

"Ah, huh," was all Bill said in response. After emptying all the cans, we decided it was time to clean them. Picking up trash and scrubbing cans was not the magical Zen experience that mopping the cafeteria had been. Instead of clearing my head, it mostly made me want to gag.

The gym doors opened, and the football team ran onto the field for practice. I tried not to look at them. Why did we have to wash the cans out here? I sighed and grabbed the next one. Bill followed my gaze to the field. "John says the team is hurting since you left."

"Who's John?" I asked.

Bill pulled a Red Bull out of his back pocket and leaned against the wall. "Coach Hughes. We go way back, you know?"

"Oh, yeah?"

"Never been a big football fan myself, but I like watching the games with John because he screams at the television. It's always good for a laugh." When I didn't say anything, he continued, "I saw the video of you giving that kid a once-over. I guess everybody did."

I kicked a can over to let the water run out into the grass.

"I shouldn't say this because fighting ain't the answer," Bill said, "and John would kill me...but he appreciates how you stuck up for Frances, and so do I."

Even though I was holding a nasty garbage can, and sweat poured down the side of my face, I smiled a little, oddly pleased to know that Bill approved. "Thanks."

We hung outside the gym while the football team ran drills, cracking jokes whenever anyone fumbled or fell.

He told me stories about how he and Coach stole the driver's ed car in high school only to crash it into a lamp post five minutes later and flee the scene.

"They couldn't prove it was us, but somehow everyone knew. We spent the rest of the year with Principal Lewis crammed up our behinds."

"Sounds uncomfortable," I said and carried one of the cans inside the gym. "Did Coach's wife go to high school with you guys, too?"

"Linda? No, John met Linda in college." He took the can out of my hands and set it down in front of him to put a new liner on. "Why do you ask?"

"No reason." I was lying, but I wasn't sure how to ask what I wanted to know.

"What is it?" he asked, sensing my hesitation.

"Uh...did she always have a problem?"

Bill didn't look at me as he put the lid on the can and smacked the top to keep it in place. "What do you mean?"

I should have kept my mouth shut, but there was no way to take it back now. I didn't know why I cared anyway, other than it mattered to Frances. "You know," I said, lowering my voice. "*A drinking problem.*"

Bill's mouth formed a thin line. "It's not a dirty secret kid. Anyway, who told you that?"

"Frances."

Bill rubbed the back of his neck. "Frances is a good kid, but she's like me: plays her cards close to her chest." He looked at me with a small, sideways smile. "She must trust you if she told you that."

I didn't know what to say, so I was grateful when Bill kept talking. "I think you're a good kid, but John and Linda are my best friends, so, I'm not going to discuss their personal business with you over a garbage can."

"Sorry," I said, and I meant it. "I shouldn't have asked."

Our usual banter dissolved as we finished putting our gear away, but before we left, Bill added, "All you need to know is that their family has been through hard times, and they're getting back on their feet." He gave me a level look. "It takes time to put things back together."

I couldn't help but think of my own damaged family. It was broken into so many pieces that I couldn't imagine there would ever be enough time to put it back together.

CHAPTER 26

Frances

The doorbell rang as I struggled through a complicated algebra equation, so I ignored it. Dad bellowed my name from downstairs, and I slammed my pencil down, annoyed at the interruption. "You know, some of us want to get into a decent college someday," I yelled as I stomped down the stairs, but when I reached the landing, the frown on Dad's face halted my progress.

"Someone to see you, Franny." It was impossible to miss his accusatory tone as he motioned to Jesse standing in the doorway. I couldn't see Dad's expression from the stairs, but Jesse looked concerned.

"Thanks," I muttered and cleared the last leg of stairs two steps at a time. I swept through the entrance, closed the door in Dad's face, and leaned against the frame. "Hey," I said the second the door was firmly latched.

"Hey," Jesse said back at me. He was wearing blue jeans, a Captain America t-shirt, and for some reason smelled like garbage.

After the initial greeting, he appeared to be trapped in an awkward loop of looking down and clearing his throat.

Curiosity got the better of me. "How did you know where I live?"

"Huh? Oh, uh, Bill dropped me off. I was helping him clean trash cans after school."

At least that explained the smell. "So, what are you doing here?"

"Well," he rubbed his neck, which looked red. I tilted my head to examine him fully. He was pretty charming when he didn't know what to say. Finally, he pulled a rolled-up paper out of his backpack and handed it to me. "I got my paper back."

I eagerly snatched it out of his hands. When I saw the grade, I smiled and whispered a happy, "Oh," as I sat down on the front steps. "I knew she would love it. Blackwell is a sucker for a good feminist theory."

Jesse sat down next to me. "Thanks to you," he said. "I never would have gotten that grade on my own."

"Not true," I said. "You're a terrific writer. You just didn't know it."

"I never really tried before. I was never good at anything but football." His eyes were amazing up close. They danced like he was laughing even when he was being serious.

"Well, now you do," I said, unable to take my gaze off him.

He leaned forward and my heart screeched to a dead stop. *He's going to kiss me.* I felt the heat from his closeness on my skin. I didn't even mind that he smelled like a dumpster.

The sound of a slamming screen door broke the spell, and we both pulled away in a hurry.

Ms. Weary walked out her front door to water her roses. I closed my eyes and silently cursed my elderly neighbor into an overdue grave. She noticed us and snorted a phlegmy grunt of disapproval. I waved at her, but as usual, she turned her back on me as if I didn't exist.

Jesse watched this exchange with interest. "What's with her?"

"Oh, that's just Ms. Weary. She hates us."

Jesse raised an eyebrow. "Why does she hate you?"

"Well, for starters, she's just mean. But let's just say she's seen my family at our worst."

Jesse gave me a questioning look, prompting me to continue.

I sighed, knowing there was no good way to spin this. "When my mom was drinking, she'd come home late. Sometimes we'd call the cops, or the cops would find her and bring her home. Sometimes she'd make a scene." I was right; it sounded worse when I said it out loud. "I'm afraid we have a bit of a reputation in the neighborhood."

Jesse looked thoughtfully at my neighbors' house. "So, because of the things your mom did, she's mean to *you*?"

I shrugged. "I don't really care."

Jesse didn't say anything more about Ms. Weary. Instead, he reached into his pocket and pulled out another piece of paper.

He dropped one of Sonny's flyers into my lap, and my face burned with mortification. "Oh, that."

He examined me thoughtfully. "So, if you don't really want to be queen, why are you doing this?"

I didn't know what to say and my mouth opened and closed several times trying to come up with an appropriate response.

Jesse looked like he wanted to laugh. "Don't answer that. I don't think I want to know." He stood up, and so did I, although I hoped my disappointment didn't show on my face.

"See you at school, Frances." He made his way down the porch stairs.

I took a deep breath to calm my frayed nerves. "Why do you keep calling me Frances?"

I knew I wasn't going to get a reasonable answer when his eyes sparkled back at me the way they did.

"Because that's your name," he said, and he waved as he headed down the drive. All I could do was watch him go, confused but unable to keep from smiling.

CHAPTER 27

Jesse

My alarm went off at three in the morning, and I rolled over to silence it before it woke Mom. I groaned and swung my legs around the side of the bed, groping for my shoes. There was no time to wait for my eyes to open. I had to move fast if I was going to get there and back before Mom realized I was gone. I didn't bother throwing on another shirt. I grabbed the supplies I needed, which were wrapped in a garbage bag under my bed, and crept out of the house, careful not to make any noise as I clicked the door shut.

I stole through the sleeping neighborhood, sticking to the side of the road and out of the streetlights in case any early risers spotted me. When I reached my first stop, I worked quickly in the dark.

For some reason, I couldn't keep Dad out of my mind. He would be so mad if he knew what I was doing. I reminded myself it didn't matter what he thought anymore, but the feeling of his disapproval was hard to shake.

Once I finished my first task, I loaded the garbage bag and flung it over my shoulder. There was limited time to get to the school and back if I was going to beat the sunrise, so I jogged there to make up some time.

Bill's heavy key ring snagged in my pocket when I tried to pull it out, but I breathed a sigh of relief when the lock turned and clicked free. I knew he wouldn't let me down. Inside the school, I looked down the dark hallway to make sure things were clear. Bill promised no one would be there this early, but I doubted that adding breaking and entering on top of suspension and being kicked off the team would look good on a college admission form.

It was strange being at school when no one else was around. It felt surreal, like one of those dreams where you're giving a speech to the entire school and realize you're naked. I quickly made my way down the hallway, eager to finish and get home.

With my mission complete, I stashed the remaining garbage bags and tools by the dumpster and ran most of the way home. The sun was peaking over the tops of the houses when my feet hit the driveway, and I grabbed the newspaper on my way in.

Mom was already in the kitchen making coffee. She looked up, startled when she heard the door. "Were you outside? Why are you so sweaty?"

Lying to Mom was all about telling part of the truth. If I straight-up lied to her, she could smell it. I placed the paper on the counter. "I was running."

She raised an eyebrow. "Running?"

I shrugged and gave her my best, "Oh, Mom," look. "I'm not playing football anymore." I pointed out. "I got to stay in shape somehow." I sat down at the counter and smiled. "Got any eggs?" I was as cool and relaxed as I could be under her gaze. I figured if I got away with this, maybe I'd take drama next year.

She eyed me, but her face softened into a smile as she poured her coffee. "I'll make some."

CHAPTER 28

Frances

"Good morning!" sang Naomi as she danced over to our lockers, twirling in clumsy silhouettes. "It's a marvelous day, isn't it?"

I glanced at Trevor. "What's with her?"

"Mr. Wonderful, who else?" he replied in a droll tone.

"Ah," I said with a smile. Although I still didn't agree with her tactics, it was nice to see Naomi so happy, as delusional and misguided as she was. "So?" I asked, "How is the master plan progressing?"

Naomi quickly pulled out her phone and showed me a text Webb sent her the night before: *Hey, Naomi. This is Webb from the interview. I was wondering if you could tell me when the paper is going to run the story about my poem? Thanks.*

I looked between her and the phone. "What did you tell him?"

"I told him it would run in the next issue." She was still grinning like a fool as I tried to think of a way to pose my question without sounding condescending, but I'm not sure I managed it.

"Naomi, don't you think it's going to be awkward when the paper comes out and there's no article?"

She shrugged dismissively. "The paper doesn't come out until after prom. He will be madly in love with me by then, and it won't matter, anyway." She opened her locker and shoved some books in. "I'll bet he finds the whole thing hysterical."

Trevor and I exchanged loaded glances that said we weren't so sure about that. Yet, we also knew better than to argue with her.

Trevor turned to me. "And what about you?"

I cast Trevor some side-eye as I worked the combination to my locker. "What about me?"

"Don't play dumb," he scolded. "Naomi told me *all* about your little date. I can't believe I'm the last to know."

I eyed him warily, hoping he wasn't planning on making a big deal out of nothing.

"You haven't exactly been available," I pointed out. Lately, Trevor had been ditching on plans and barely returning messages. When Naomi tried to talk to him about it, he brushed it off as being busy with schoolwork or the campaign. "Anyway, it wasn't a date." I cursed under my breath when my locker combination refused to give.

"That's not what I heard," he said. "I don't suppose you've considered what going out with Jesse could do for your campaign? Pretty crafty; he's been nominated for king. If he wins, you two could be a real power couple."

I dropped the stupid lock and it banged against the locker door. "Trevor, I did *not* go out with Jesse so I could be prom queen."

"Ha! So, you admit it was a date." He cast me a smug look.

I rolled my eyes. "Whatever, Sherlock Holmes."

"Fine, don't tell me about it. I'll just get all the gory details from the man himself."

My neck snapped around. "Trevor, don't you dare say *anything*."

Naomi frowned. "Come on, Trev. Leave her alone."

"What?" His tone would've sounded hurt to anyone who didn't know him like I did. "If she doesn't want to spill the juice about her date, that's fine. I'll just acquire the intel from other reliable sources." His eyes were positively sparkling with the thrill of winding me up.

I took a deep breath because I knew a big reaction was what he was after, but if he didn't shut his mouth soon, I was dangerously close to shutting it for him. My face must have shown my irritation because Trevor grinned wider.

"Oh my," he said, "she's really angry, isn't she Naomi?"

Naomi bit her lip and glanced between us.

I worked my locker combination again and tried to ignore him. When he realized I wasn't going to take the bait, he backed off a little. "Okay, Franny, don't blow a gasket. If you don't want to talk about your date, I'm not going to make you."

The lock came free, and I sighed. Trevor had a way of getting under people's skin, even while admitting defeat. "It...wasn't...a...*date*," I said and yanked my locker door open.

A shower of color fell all around me. Hundreds of yellow roses came pouring from my locker, covering my head and the floor.

The three of us stared, awestruck at the pile of flowers laying at our feet.

Students on their way to class stopped to stare at the bewildering site. "What the...?" I muttered and plucked one of the delicate blossoms from the floor. I looked at Trevor and Naomi, surprised to see a sea of dumbfounded faces. "Did either of you—"

"No." Naomi lightly touched the rose in my hand with her fingertips.

"Sorry, kid," said Trevor. "I haven't a clue." As I turned the rose over in my hand, he said, "It's not exactly a prank. It's..."

"Beautiful," I finished, a little breathless.

The bell rang, which snapped me out of my stupor. The hallway started to clear, and when I turned around, Jesse was leaning against the wall of lockers across the hall, a lopsided grin on his face. Holy crap. Had he been there the whole time?

"Not a date, huh?" Trevor whispered in my ear before tactfully slipping off to class, but I barely registered his words. No one had ever given me flowers before, and I had no idea what to say.

Jesse seemed to sense this because he winked at me, pushed off the wall, and silently strolled down the hallway.

I was late to my first class because I stayed behind to clean up the flowers. Sadly, I had to get rid of most of them because there was no reasonable way to take them home. Still, I slipped a single perfect rose inside the front pocket of my bookbag.

My first three classes were a blur as I fumbled my way from subject to subject. By the time I got to science class, all I could think about was what I was going to say to Jesse. How could I find the right combination of words to tell him how wonderful and crazy his gesture was? Then, of course, there was the ever-looming question: *Why?*

Mrs. McGee was going over the review for next week's test, and I was trying to concentrate on my notes when Naomi nudged my arm. I looked at her, and she smiled. Despite the familiar voice telling me never to get my hopes up, I couldn't help but smile back as we both silently acknowledged what the roses could mean.

In a great show of tact not generally found in her, Naomi kept quiet on the way to lunch, and I was grateful. Already, my stomach was a pit of nerves.

Trevor and Chris were already engrossed in a heated debate about whether Ironman or Batman was the better non-mutant superhero, and they barely waved when we got to the table. I wanted to interrupt them and ask where Jesse was, but I looked around and realized he wasn't the only one missing. "Where's Sonny?"

Everyone shrugged, but I didn't have time to wonder because my phone chimed with a text from Jesse: *Hey. Had to help Bill unload new desks. Meet me after school?*

My heartbeat sped up. *Where?* I replied.

Main entrance.

I wanted to ask why, but figured I'd find out soon enough. *Okay, I'll be there.*

Awesome, he replied.

Trevor and Chris didn't notice our lack of participation in their debate, which went on way too long. Naomi mentioned that her mom and brother got into a fight the night before. Naomi's brother getting into trouble was one of her favorite subjects.

"Apparently, Ron managed to flunk half his classes at FSU, and I overheard Mom say that if he doesn't clean his grades up, she's going to stop paying his tuition." Naomi relayed this information with the bare minimum of sisterly sympathy. Ron was goofy and sarcastic, and he was always good for a laugh, particularly when it was at Naomi's expense.

"Well, I'm sure he will get things straightened out," I said.

"Not likely. You know Ron; he doesn't take anything seriously. I'm sure we'll be seeing him when he comes home crying to Mom."

Trying to get Naomi to cut Ron some slack was a pointless endeavor. "Well, tell him I said hi when you talk to him."

Naomi shrugged. "Whatever."

Sonny finally walked up, hauling a large garbage bag over her shoulder. Everyone's conversations stopped as she plopped the bag on the table and sat down. It stank like rotting food and old grease.

"Jeez, Sonny, were you dumpster diving?" asked Naomi as she tried to stifle a gag.

Sonny said nothing, but her satisfied smile said she was more than a little pleased with her haul. I glanced inside the bag. It was mostly garbage but there was some metal wire, and what looked like red and blue floral window coverings. "Are those the curtains from the teacher's lounge?" I spotted a maggot trying to complete a migration from the bag to the table. "Maybe you should put this on the floor," I suggested.

Sonny shrugged and removed it.

"Why do you have this stuff, anyway?" Trevor asked.

But she ignored our questions and slipped her headphones over her ears, a clear sign we were on a need-to-know basis.

THE REST of the day passed in a rush of forgotten books and always being three steps behind. I barely paid attention in math, and I spent the entire break between classes trying to get notes from someone.

As I rushed down the hall, someone came tearing around the

corner and crashed into me. All my books and carefully organized binders scattered across the hall. I closed my eyes and took a deep breath, trying to calm my simmering annoyance.

I bent down and barely acknowledged the person as they tried to help gather up my stuff.

"Sorry, I didn't see you," said a low voice.

I snatched a book from their hand, feeling my temper flare.

"Forget it," I snapped. "It's just one of those days."

But when I glanced up, Nick Temple was crouched on the floor beside me.

Nick and I hadn't said two words to each other since middle school that wasn't an insult, and now I watched as he gingerly gathered my books and papers off the floor and handed them to me. "Thank you," I said, my voice barely audible.

He nodded, meeting my eyes for only an instant before he got up and walked away, leaving me wondering if this day could get any more bizarre.

———

NICK WAS STILL on my mind when the final bell rang. I tried to remember the last time I'd seen him. He was usually the type that ate up lots of attention from everyone around him—begrudgingly, myself included.

Students filled the courtyard. I still wasn't used to how people smiled and waved at me: a lingering side-effect of Trevor's and Sonny's dramatic flyer campaign. I had to admit, the vast cavern of space I'd once felt between myself and everyone else in school had become smaller.

"You okay?" Jesse asked.

I jumped, torn away from my private reflection. Most of the students were gone, and I wondered how long I had been standing there. "Sorry, just thinking."

"Must have been heavy stuff; you look pretty serious."

I felt like my awkwardness and Nick's social welfare were likely tough subjects to tackle for now, so I just shrugged.

"Want to go somewhere with me?" he asked.

"Depends on where we are going." I hoped for levity, but I think I just sounded suspicious.

"The football field. Nothing creepy, I promise."

I made an unintelligible noise and grabbed my bookbag. "Sounds magical."

"Well, I do know how to show a girl a good time."

His joke fell flat, and we walked toward the gym in awkward silence. We passed Bill on the way as he scraped paint off an old bench in the courtyard. Jesse called out to him, and Bill gave us a thumbs up and a knowing smile that made me blush and duck my head.

We walked through the gym and headed out back toward the field. I rarely came out this way unless I was helping Dad. A couple of the guys waved at Jesse as they ran from one end of the field to the other.

"Don't miss that," he muttered as we ascended the bleachers.

We were headed to the highest row of seats. As I stepped over a bench to reach the last aisle, Jesse automatically took my hand to help me over it. When I looked down, Dad was watching us from the field.

We sat down and watched the team practice for a while.

"I like to come here sometimes," he explained.

It occurred to me that he might be nervous. Unfortunately, sarcasm is pretty much how I deal with everything. "Yeah, nice and peaceful watching a bunch of guys bash into each other."

He looked at me.

I bit my lip. "I suppose it's peaceful. When no one else is here."

I glanced out at the field then back at him. "Does it bother you?"

He raised an eyebrow questioningly.

"Not being on the team anymore," I clarified.

"At first, yeah. I mean, sometimes." Jesse shrugged. "Do you go to games?"

"I used to, but only when Dad needed help with equipment or something. It's not my favorite thing to do."

He nodded, and there was another awkward break in the conversation. I'd been hoping he'd bring up the flowers so I wouldn't have to, but it became clear that he wasn't going to, so I decided it was now or never. "Do I want to know how you got into my locker?"

At least he had the decency to look a little guilty. "Probably not."

"I thought they were amazing," I said.

A slow smile spread across his features, and the tips of his ears turned a little pink. "You like to read," he said out of nowhere, and I blinked at the rapid subject change.

"All the time."

"What's your favorite book?"

"Sorry," I said seriously. "Can't tell you that."

"Yeah?" he asked, looking more interested. "How come?"

"Because it's super cliché."

He raised both eyebrows, but his eyes danced. "So, just tell me."

"Sorry, not happening," I said with a shrug. I wondered if this was what people meant by flirting. I'd never consciously done it before, and I decided it was a question worth tabling for deeper reflection.

"Is it, like, romance stuff?"

I scoffed at his assumption. "Because I'm a girl, right?"

He grinned and didn't look at all shamed. "Because you're a romantic person."

Of all the words I'd use to describe myself, *romantic* had never been on my list. "I don't know what you're talking about," I said honestly.

His eyes met mine and for a second, I felt lost in them. "You would, if you had seen your face when you got the flowers."

Heat flooded my cheeks, and I looked down at the field, suddenly fascinated with everything in that direction.

He sat quietly beside me and shifted his foot over the dirty bleacher. "I didn't mean to embarrass you."

I shook my head but still couldn't look at him. I wanted to run, kiss him, and punch him in the face all at the same time. "*Pride and Prejudice*," I said.

When he didn't respond, I finally met his eyes again. "It's my favorite book."

He grinned, accepting my acknowledgement that he was right, but too generous to point it out. "Looks like the team is heading in."

Hurried and nervous, I started talking before I knew what I was saying. "Do you need a lift? You can catch a ride with Dad and me."

"Thanks, but your dad doesn't look happy with me right now."

He was right. Dad stood on the sidelines, hands on his hips, watching us from the field. I rolled my eyes and silently cursed him for being so weird.

Jesse grinned and stood up, taking my hand without warning. "Want to make him crazy?"

I gaped as he pulled me into a standing position. "What are you doing?"

Gingerly, Jesse brought his lips down to the top of my hand. They felt cool at first, then warm. I wondered for a millisecond how they would feel on my lips. My mouth must have been open the entire time; he'd managed to dazzle me twice in the same day. "See you around, Frances."

JESSE HAD BEEN RIGHT. Dad was not happy on the ride home. He demanded to know what Jesse and I were doing, and I was grateful Jesse hadn't taken me up on my offer of a lift. "You should know," I said, my voice tainted with sarcasm. "You were spying on us the whole time."

"I don't like that tone, Franny," he said sourly.

I shrugged and glanced out the window. "You're overreacting."

"But wha—" Dad stopped talking as we pulled closer to the house. "Now what the hell is going on?"

I followed Dad's gaze to the police car parked in front of our house, and my heart lurched at the memory of Mom being helped out of the back of a cruiser. That night she could barely walk, but she still had enough energy to slur obscenities to anyone within a two-block radius.

When I opened the car door, I heard Ms. Weary speaking—or rather yelling—at a very flustered young police officer. She made wild hand gestures, and her normal pasty complexion was alive with rage. "How can you just stand there?" she demanded of the officer. "They stole all my beautiful roses!"

I looked down at her garden, and sure enough the heads of all her roses had been lopped clean off, leaving only the barren, headless stems. My heart thudded to a stop. "He didn't," I murmured incredulously.

Dad looked at me. "Did you say something?"

I shook my head, maybe a little too hard, and pushed the yellow rose deeper into my bag's front pocket. "Nope, but who can hear anything with Weary screaming?" I hurried into the house.

CHAPTER 29

Jesse

"Did you order the pizza yet?" asked Lucy from the living room. "I'm only starving to death over here."

In the kitchen, Chris and I were glued to our phones as we searched for coupon codes. We hoped for a magic discount that would grant us free bread sticks or wings, anything to maximize the forty bucks his parents left us while watching Lucy.

"We're working on it," yelled Chris.

"But you guys have been in there for a half hour," she whined. "Just pick something already. You know I have low blood sugar!"

"*Jeez*, kid," snapped Chris. "Why don't you get lost or something?"

Lucy turned from her cartoons and leaned over the back of the couch to glower at us.

We were stuck watching Lucy because she'd chased off all her other babysitters. The last one left in tears because Lucy convinced her that her dream of attending Harvard was, in her expert opinion, "doomed to fail" because she didn't have the refined sophistication Harvard recruiters look for. The girl ended up going to a local college. After that, all the other babysitters were booked when Chris's parents wanted to go out.

Personally, I always liked hanging out with Lucy. The fact that she annoyed Chris was just a bonus. I winked at her from behind the counter. "We're almost done, Einstein."

Her irritated expression melted into a bright smile. "Did you know after Einstein died, they cut up his brain and found out it was denser than most other human brains?"

"Nobody cares, freak," cut in Chris before I could respond. "Ha!" He brandished his phone in front of him as if it were Excalibur. "Free breadsticks and twenty percent off!"

"You're the master," I said.

Lucy rolled her eyes and turned back to the television. She muttered something under her breath that sounded like the word *imbeciles*.

Chris submitted the order and hopped on the counter. "That was exhausting."

"Fiscal responsibility is no joke." My pocket vibrated, and I pulled out my phone. It was a message notification from Dad. Normally, I'd send all his texts directly to the trash, but after staring at it for a second, I tapped it open.

Jesse, I miss you and I want us to talk soon. There's a lot to say. I didn't want to say this in a text, but Kim and I found out we're having a girl...

I quickly hit the trash icon and shoved my phone back in my pocket. I took a deep breath and let it out slowly to let my anger dissipate before anyone noticed. "So," I said, hoping to sound casual, "I was thinking I'd ask Frances to prom."

"You really think she'd go with you?" Chris shot back.

I frowned at his doubtful expression. "Didn't realize I was so un-dateable."

"Well, she likes you for sure, especially after that flower stunt you pulled. Why did you do that, anyway? I mean, it was kind of weird."

"It wasn't that weird."

"Well," Chris smirked, "you never did anything like that for Sarah."

"Sarah's allergic to flowers."

Chris smirked at my evasion. "You know what I mean."

When I still didn't answer, Chris rubbed his chin with his thumb and forefinger, putting on his most distinguished and thoughtful pose. When he spoke, it was in a terrible British accent that fell somewhere between Shakespeare and the Count from *Sesame Street.* "Perhaps thy feelings for the lady may yet overcome thy ugly face, so she may yet accept your proposal of prom."

"Lucy's right," I said. "You're an imbecile."

He made a motion to tip an imaginary top hat in my direction. "Quite."

I grabbed a dish towel from the counter and flung it at his face, and he laughed. "So, you going to do one of those crazy 'prom-posal' deals? Get down on one knee or make matching t-shirts?"

"I don't have a death wish. She'd murder me and feed my body to fire ants if I did something like that."

"You think she'd go that easy on you?"

Suddenly, Lucy's hand slammed down on the counter, and we both jumped. With a flourish, she raised her hand to reveal a folded piece of paper with little hearts drawn on the outside.

I picked up the paper. "What's this?"

"I crunched the numbers and came up with the percentage likelihood of Frances going to prom with you," Lucy said.

I grinned and turned the paper over in my hand. "Lucy, asking someone out isn't a math equation you can work out on paper."

"*Jesse.*" She took on the stern tone of a teacher correcting a particularly slow student. "The entirety of the universe, how it was formed and where it is going, can be explained with a single elegant equation."

"So?" I prompted, even though I had a feeling she was about to insult me.

"So," she continued, "if scientists can do that, I think I can figure the odds of you getting a date."

Lucy was just a kid. A *really* smart kid, but not someone I would take dating advice from. Still, I unfolded the paper to reveal a series of long equations scrawled in bubbly letters. At the bottom of the string of variables was the percentage circled with a heart.

"*Thirty-eight percent?*" I said indignantly.

"There is a small margin of error, but yes, I'm afraid so," she replied.

Chris hopped off the counter and looked at the paper over my shoulder. "Don't pay any attention to her. Someday her species will return to this planet to take her back where she belongs."

Lucy ignored her brother. "I calculated the likelihood she would respond favorably to your invitation based on the number of positive and negative responses you've said she's given you in the past. I've also taken into consideration the likelihood that she would want to attend a prom-like event with you based on her age, demographic, and current geographical social trends. It's all very precise."

Chris snatched the paper from me and waved it in Lucy's face. "Precise, my butt. This is written in pink gel pen."

Lucy shrugged. "Just trying to save you the shame of being turned down."

"Whatever, Lucy," I said, a little more annoyed than I was willing to admit. I turned to Chris. "What about you? Taking anyone?"

Chris blew out a long breath and crossed his arms over the back of his head. "Oh, you know. Just got to decide who deserves the honor of taking me."

"What about Naomi?" I asked. I thought that if Chris took Naomi, Frances might be more open to going with me. But then again, I'd yet to see Frances do anything she didn't really want to.

"Naomi, as in, Naomi?" he asked, looking surprised.

"Yeah. How many other Naomis do we know?"

"I thought she was going with some guy named Webb."

Frances told me she wanted to go with him but wasn't sure if that was going to work out. "You never know," I said. "If Webb doesn't take her, she's going to need a fallback guy."

"Awesome," Chris said with a thin smile. "Just call me fallback guy. Does that come with a cape?"

"Don't take it personal; it's just a suggestion. It's not like you have a date yet, anyway."

Chris looked like he was about to argue, but Lucy interrupted him.

"Yeah. right," she said with a droll snort. "I don't need any calculations to know Chris's chances of getting a date. *Zero*."

Her brother glared at her. "Shut up, troll."

Lucy folded her arms across her chest. "Calling me names isn't going to get you guys dates." She turned her back on us and sauntered back into the living room. "Numbers don't lie, gentlemen. Call me when the pizza gets here."

CHAPTER 30

Frances

I greeted people on my way to class, which seemed to be the new custom. I honestly couldn't say I was friends with any of them, but I was now loose acquaintances with almost everyone at school. This led to a slight easing of tightness in my chest when walking down the hall. The faint glow of acceptance was sweet, although I questioned why I felt like I needed it.

Walking on pillowed clouds of unfiltered bliss always mucks up my thinking. For the first time, I felt like it might be possible that Jesse Harmon was interested in me. *And why not?* I wondered. I was, after all, well on my way to becoming West Pine High's next prom queen. That thought, absurd as it was, hit me so hard that I almost buckled with laughter. However, a glance at any wall in school told a different story. Colorful depictions of me, more variations of the original flyer, had been posted everywhere. With new slogans, the flyers hung in lockers and were used as a background image on cell phone screens. Trevor even had t-shirts made. It's a strange thing to see your face on the back of someone you don't even know. Somehow my likeness had become a fashion trend.

This idea—combined with thoughts of prom, Jesse's goofy smile, and the feel of his lips on the top of my hand—distracted me until a conversation loud enough to rise above the hallway chatter captured my attention.

Two large guys several lockers away were practically yelling, their voices irritated. The tall one wore a varsity football shirt.

"I can't believe Harmon screwed us like this." He smacked his locker with his forearm, causing his friend to jump.

"Maybe Coach will change his mind," offered his friend weakly.

"Harmon wasn't that great of a quarterback anyway, but at least he kept Mike on the bench. Let's just hope Mike learns how to throw by next year."

I frowned, wondering which Mike they were talking about. I wasn't even sure why I cared. I doubted those two could find anything nice to say about anyone. I turned toward my locker, fully prepared to ignore them for the rest of my life, when I heard one of them say, "Hey, there she is."

I froze in place. *They aren't talking about you*, I told myself. *Just get your books and leave.*

"Come on, Greg," said the smaller of the two, his voice ringing out with a slight chuckle. "She'll hear you."

"Who cares?" said the tall one.

I quickly pulled a book from my locker and buried my face in it, pretending to read.

"Look at her," he said, not bothering to hide the disgust in his voice. "Even I couldn't pretend to be into *that* just to weasel my way back on the team."

My whole body tensed. I glanced at them, appalled to see them both staring at me. I wanted to rail at them and tell them it wasn't true, but a sudden rush of bile scorched the back of my throat. It couldn't be true. Jesse had defended me, hadn't he? The events of the past few weeks replayed in my head: the movie, the flowers, when he said he wasn't good at anything besides football...

Finally, after what seemed like hours of listening to them make jokes at my expense, the bell rang. They left, but their laughter still rung in my ears. I leaned against the locker and released the air trapped in my lungs, but it didn't lessen the ache in my chest, or stop cold tears from streaking my cheeks.

CHAPTER 31

Jesse

"Has anyone seen Frances?" The cafeteria was packed because they'd crammed all the lunches together so everyone could go to the pep rally at three. I wanted to convince Frances to ditch with me, but she hadn't shown up for lunch.

Neither Trevor nor Naomi had seen her, and Sonny didn't respond at all. I waved a hand in front of her face, but she still didn't glance up from her tablet. I made the mistake of tapping her on the shoulder, and she nearly jumped out of her seat.

I raised both hands in self-defense. "Whoa, sorry. I was just wondering if you'd seen Frances."

Sonny's expression softened, but she still lightly brushed at the spot where I'd touched her. Instead of answering my question, she flipped her tablet around and showed me what she was working on. It was another picture of Frances, but this time she stood straight, hands on her hips, her intense look penetrating the screen. I almost laughed because this kind of pose wouldn't have been hard to get out of Frances. Sonny superimposed another set of wings to her back, but these were blood red and black with a backdrop of fire that made Frances look ferocious. I loved it.

"Well, you've captured her spirit, Sonny. That's for sure."

She smiled and turned back to her work. I sent Frances a quick text, but when I didn't see an immediate response, I tried to eat my lunch and follow along with the conversation. She usually replied fast, and I wondered if something was going on with her mom. I could go see if Coach was in his office to ask him if he knew where she was, but I sacked the idea right away. I wouldn't say he was gunning for me exactly, but judging by the suspicious looks he'd been throwing at me, I didn't think he'd be overly concerned if his daughter wasn't taking my calls.

The food on my plate didn't interest me, so I told everyone I'd catch up with them later. With everyone at lunch, the hallway was quiet, and the only sound was the occasional door opening or closing in distant hallways. It made me think about the night I'd snuck in to shove the flowers in Frances's locker. I hadn't gotten caught, but even if I had, the look on her face would have made it worth it. That was what I was thinking about when I turned the corner and crashed right into her.

She lost her balance, but I grabbed her arm to steady her. "Jeez, you okay?"

"Yeah," she said and took her arm back. "I'm fine."

I smiled like an idiot. I was that happy to see her. "Where've you been? I texted you, and when you didn't show up to lunch, I thought something was wrong."

She didn't explain. Instead, she just said, "I was busy."

"Oh." I wanted to press her, but something about her tone made me back off. "You sure everything's okay?"

She didn't say anything, and I realized why she looked so weird. No matter how hard I tried to catch her eye, she refused to look at me. I fought the urge to take her hand by stuffing mine in my pockets. "Come on, Frances. What's up?"

The awkward silence that followed was almost unbearable, so I did the absolute dumbest thing ever. "Listen." I took my hand from my pocket and ran it over the back of my neck. A pool of sweat formed at the base, so I covertly wiped it on my shirt. "I wanted to ask you something. I mean, I know you'll probably think it's lame, but I was thinking maybe we could go to—"

"Just stop," she blurted out.

I stared at her. "What?"

She finally looked at me, but her eyes were hard. "Do you think I'm stupid?"

"Do I—what are you talking about?"

Her voice rose higher, and her cheeks flamed with bright color. "Whatever game you're playing, it needs to end."

I had no idea what she was talking about, but panic rose inside me, like I was about to be pushed in front of a speeding train.

"You know," she said into my stunned silence, "I almost fell for it, but I should have known you were just like the rest of them: too worried about your next big play to consider how you might hurt other people."

I crossed my arms over my chest, not thrilled with her brutal summary of my character. "How about you just tell me what it is you think I've done?"

She closed her eyes for a second, and when she opened them, her stare was cold and resolved. "I know you've only been hanging out with me to get back on the team, *okay*? It didn't work, so it's time to drop the game and admit you've lost."

My mouth fell open. About a million comebacks ran through my head, but I was too pissed to say any of them. Did she really believe that? "Sounds like you have it all figured out."

For a second, I thought I saw real pain flash across her face, but she schooled her features into a steel look which only flared my temper. "Admit that you care about me," I said.

Her eyes widened, and her face burned brighter. Although she hadn't *technically* said that she liked me, the outrage in her eyes told me what we both already knew.

"I don't," she insisted. "Maybe if you weren't so full of yourself, you'd know that."

The things she said were more than just letters and words. They instantly evoked the disappointment of a blown throw on the last game of the season or the pain of when Dad walked out on us. I stared down at her, this girl who was so willing to stomp my heart into a million pieces. "Full of myself? This from someone who launched an entire campaign just to get people to like her. Frances, you're just as self-serving and superficial as everyone else. At least they're not pretending to be something they're not."

She recoiled as if I'd hit her, and her eyes sparkled with tears. In a whisper barely loud enough to hear, she said, "I hate you, Jesse Harmon."

CHAPTER 32

Frances

When I turned the corner, Sonny walked out of the cafeteria. She shot down the hallway like a rocket when she saw me, her bookbag bouncing off her back in noisy bursts.

I held up a hand and used the other to swipe at the gathering tears in my eyes. "Not a good time," I said.

She skidded to a stop in front of me, but her excited expression didn't fade as she drew her iPad out of her bag and revealed yet another prom poster made from my likeness. This time I was surrounded by what looked like fire and brimstone. Although it was a decent reflection of how I felt, I couldn't bring myself to smile at it.

"I said, not now." I tried to push past her, but she followed close behind. Why couldn't she just leave me alone for once? I turned around. "Don't you get it, Sonny? This whole thing is a joke."

Sonny blinked at me, clearly not understanding. Frustrated, I ripped one of my posters off the wall, the colorful paper tearing at the corners. "I'm not going to be prom queen, okay? I quit."

"Excuse me?" demanded Trevor's angry voice behind me.

I whirled around. My face must have been a mess because Trevor and Naomi both took a step back, their expressions marked with shock.

"Frances, what's wrong?" asked Naomi.

"What's wrong?" I repeated, my voice shrill. "I'm done." I crumbled the flyer in my fist and let it fall to the floor. "I won't be a joke anymore." I could feel fresh tears gathering, but I willed them to keep from spilling over my cheeks.

Trevor frowned. "Did something happen with Jesse? We just saw him, but he wouldn't stop to talk to us."

I closed my eyes against the sound of his name. I tried to stay calm, but my chest hurt with each shuddering breath.

"Did you guys fight?" Naomi pushed, and I almost choked in response.

A fight? "Damnit, Naomi, it must be fantastic living in a fairytale."

"Fairytale..." Her shocked expression would have been comical if I wasn't so angry.

"I'm not going to prom," I said firmly.

Trevor held his hands up. "Wait a second, Franny." I wanted to slap the look of concern right off his face. "If you're worried about prom, Chris told me Jesse was goin—"

"No," I snapped, knowing what he was going to say. "Jesse and I are *not* going to prom together." I hated looking into their worried expressions, so I turned away only to be confronted with Sonny's wide, sad eyes.

Trevor closed the distance between us and turned me around to face him. "Franny. What the hell did you do?"

I jerked my arm away and glared at him. "What did *I* do? It was all a joke, Trevor. Are you happy now?"

He closed his eyes and shook his head. "Start from the beginning."

I quickly recounted what I'd heard in the hall this morning, all the while ignoring their appalled looks and declarations of disbelief.

"Franny, Jesse wouldn't do that," Naomi tried to argue, but romantics like her couldn't understand a story where the heroine doesn't find true love.

"He was never interested in me."

With a stark frown, Naomi crossed her arms. "I don't believe that."

"Of course, you don't," I said. "Why would you believe your best friend over someone you met a few weeks ago?"

Naomi looked at me for a long time and let out a breath. "You know, I thought you were getting better."

My head was beginning to ache. "What the hell does that mean?"

"All you ever do is think about yourself."

"Excuse me?" Was she serious? My life was falling apart, and she was telling me how self-centered I was?

"Don't act like you don't know what I'm talking about. Poor Frances," she mocked. "*She's* an outcast. Nobody *ever* understands her. Meanwhile, you have friends who love you, an entire school dying to make you prom queen, and this great guy who bends over backwards just to make you happy. But you're too hung up on what other people think to appreciate any of it."

"That's no—"

"And what about all the work we've done?" accused Trevor, giving me zero room for rebuttal. "Sonny and I have been working for weeks on your campaign, and now, when you almost have the crown in your hands, you're just giving up because your feelings got hurt?"

"Did you even once consider giving Jesse the benefit of the doubt?" Naomi interrupted, her voice rising. "At any point did you think about how much you could hurt him?"

Appalled by their tag-team and her implication that Jesse was the victim, all my emotional fortifications shot up. "Who are you to lecture me?" I asked, my whole body singing with resentment. "You're just a loser who has to lie to people so they will go out with you."

Naomi's face crumbled, and I flinched, unable to believe what I'd just said. That's the problem with mouthing off when you're angry. Once the words are out, you can't put them back in.

Without warning, Sonny was between us, holding her iPad in my face like a shield. Her voice was loud, like she didn't get she was right in front of us. "Some caterpillars protect themselves with sour tasting chemicals, so predators that attack them will be disgusted and leave them alone."

Overwhelmed by Sonny's critique on my life, and guilt over hurting Naomi, I slapped the iPad away from my face. "Knock it off!"

She lost her grip on the tablet, and it hit the floor with a terrible crunch. The screen erupted in hundreds of cracks and flittered off. Sonny shrieked and dropped to her knees.

I stared down at her, too chilled by the sight of her wailing over the shattered device to move.

Trevor dropped to the floor with her and tried to put his hand on her shoulder, but she screamed in protest.

"She doesn't like to be touched!" I yelled, but I could barely hear my own voice over the sound of Sonny's wails and the rumbling cheers of the opening pep rally.

"Just get out of here, Franny!" yelled Trevor.

I watched in horror as Sonny tried over and over to turn the device on, smacking it with jerking, panicked motions before turning her hand on herself and beating her forehead.

Too ashamed to argue, I grabbed my bookbag and ran down the hall, steeling myself against the sound of cheers from the pep rally mingled with Sonny's cries.

———

I BARELY REGISTERED my parents talking in the kitchen as I silently crept up the stairs. All I wanted to do was lock myself away, but as soon as my foot landed on the top step, mom called my name. I closed my eyes. "What?"

She was at the bottom of the stairs, practically bouncing with excitement. "I'm so glad you're home! I have some wonderful news."

Dad stepped out of the kitchen and stood beside her.

Her enthusiastic energy sent irritated tremors up my spine. Of course she was happy. Life was just a bowl of Cheerios to Mom. I glared down at them both, hoping they would get to the point so I could retreat to my room and never come out again.

"I," she paused for dramatic effect, "have been sober an entire year!" She practically sang the second half. My parents didn't exactly applaud, but they came close.

"Can you believe it? Gina is going to present me my bronze chip at the next meeting. They've asked me to speak, and I would love it if you guys were there." She leaned into Dad who wrapped an arm around her waist. They looked like the perfect couple. "I'm just so happy to b—"

"Mom, who the hell cares?" I interrupted her joyful monologue.

There were a few beats of silence as they both registered what I'd said. "What?" The dismay in her voice told me she'd heard me just fine.

"Oh, you're right. Good job not getting wasted and dumped on the front lawn for an entire year."

I could have stopped there, and my point would have been made, but the words came charging out like a verbal stampede, and they were gunning straight for her. "Oh, but wait, I forgot. What about all those great speeches you've made about your," I paused, making quote marks in the air with my fingers, "journey to sobriety." I snorted with cold, empty laughter. "You were such an inspiration all those years when the cops were peeling you off the floor of every bar in town. I'm surprised they haven't offered you the Nobel Peace Prize by now."

"*That's enough,*" Dad snapped and made a move up the stairs after me. He'd never hit me before, but instinctually I took a step back. "Apologize to your mother, *right now.*"

But now that it was out, I didn't know how to keep the anger inside anymore. I thought about all the times I'd needed her and she wasn't there, and now she wanted a pat on the back for it? I stomped halfway down the stairs and pointed a finger at her. "Screw your bronze chip!" I shouted and found some grim enjoyment in the way my words made her flinch. "You may have convinced everyone else you've changed, but you can't fool me."

Mom's face went pale. She looked at me from the bottom of the stairs like a deer staring straight into the headlights of a speeding car.

"I said that's *enough*." Dad's face was hard, but he couldn't stop the truth flowing out any more than I could.

"Dad." I turned to him, my tone imploring. "How many times did she not come home? How many times did you wonder who she was with?"

"*Frances*. Stop." Dad's voice lowered to a warning hiss.

"How many times did you let her come back like nothing happened?" Tears flowed freely down my cheeks. "Well, I can't pretend anymore! All you ever do is think about yoursel—"

Suddenly, a terrible sound filled my ears like the end of a jackhammer had been placed to the side of my temple. All the words that spilled so freely a moment ago died in my throat. I couldn't breathe, couldn't speak. Cold settled in my chest as I sunk down on the stairs. I felt like I was flowing through a current, buried beneath a thick layer of ice.

Suddenly, the coldness was smothered by warmth around my forearms, and I realized that the terrible noise was my sobbing, and the warm feeling was my mother's arms as she wrapped them around me and rocked me on the stairs.

CHAPTER 33

Jesse

For the next few days, I did my best to avoid Frances–which, of course, made me look for her everywhere. I ate lunch on the bleachers so I wouldn't run into her. That's the rhythm of breaking up with someone you don't want to break up with: you obsessively search for someone while at the same time do everything you can to avoid them. It's too bad all my search-and-avoid tactics proved pointless. Chris informed me that she hadn't been to school in days.

The breakup, if you could call it that, was not at all like my breakup with Sarah. When Sarah and I split, everyone knew about it, but I didn't care. With Frances, hardly anyone noticed because I guess we weren't technically together, yet I was completely miserable.

After our fight, I replayed our conversation in my head, trying to decrypt Frances's mysterious logic. But every time I thought about all the crappy things she'd said to me, anger clouded my thoughts. I mean, she was the reason I was kicked off in the first place, but *I* was the one who used *her*?

I walked around school like a zombie, trapped in a vicious cycle of anger and guilt. Trevor tried to speak to me a couple of times, but I refused to talk about it. I didn't want to hear about Frances. It was bad enough the entire school was wallpapered in pictures of her.

When school let out, I pushed the gym doors open to find Bill leaning against two floor buffers in the middle of the basketball court. I stood with my arms folded as he showed me how to operate the equipment, and I wondered if the school was cool with someone underage using heavy machinery. He said it would probably take us all afternoon, but I didn't care. At least I'd be busy.

I turned on the buffer and felt the hum in my hands as it came to life. Bill did the same, and we got to work. Like mopping the floors, the easy movement of labor was a welcome distraction from my thoughts.

Thankfully, Bill was the kind of guy who knew when to mind his own business. He didn't say a thing about my dark mood, and we worked in silence. It was not the same at home. Mom sensed something was up. How do mothers do that? I told her I was fine and went to my room. She didn't follow me, but every time I emerged, she asked if I was feeling okay, which was immediately followed by a pushy offer of food.

When we finished buffing the floor, Bill pulled out a set of bleachers, and we sat down. I stared at the gleaming floors and remembered a basketball game Dad had taken me to. At the time, I'd been too little to understand the rules of the game, but I loved jumping up and cheering or booing when everyone else did. There was this feeling like I knew nothing bad could happen because he was there. It's a feeling only a kid can have because they have no idea about all the horrible things life can throw at you. I swallowed a hard lump in my throat as I realized I'd never feel that way again.

A tear hit my cheek, and I quickly swiped it away on my shoulder, hoping Bill hadn't seen. If he had, he didn't say anything, but he cracked open his Red Bull and handed it to me.

CHAPTER 34

Frances

I wished I'd asked my parents to transfer me to a private school where no one knew me, but the idea of wearing one of those scratchy plaid skirts and a polo made me feel even worse. The truth was, despite my rant on the stairs, Mom and Dad hadn't made me go back to school. Mom offered to let me stay home a few more days, but I knew schoolwork was piling up. If I didn't at least go in to pick up what I'd missed, things would only get harder from there. But that wasn't the real reason either. I *needed* to see my friends, if I had any left.

Neither Trevor nor Naomi had responded to any of my calls or texts. I couldn't sleep. All I did was think about Sonny sobbing on the floor. What I'd done was unforgiveable, and I had no idea how to fix it. *Where was a time machine when a girl needed one?*

When I got to my locker, Naomi and Trevor were already there. I took a deep breath, squared my shoulders, and walked over to them. "Hey," I said, but my voice sounded more numb than confident.

Naomi pinched her lips together and turned away. Trevor cast me an irritated look and also remained silent.

"Look, guys. I get it; you're mad. But can we at least talk?"

Naomi slammed her locker shut and brushed past me as if I didn't exist.

Guess not.

"Naomi, come on." I followed behind her. "Can you at least give me a hint on how long you plan on not speaking to me?"

When she ignored my question, I opened my mouth to plead with her, but before I could, someone else called her name.

Webb Harris stood behind us. His mouth set in a hard, grim line.

"Webb," Naomi said, sounding flustered. "Hey." She forced a bright smile. "How are you?"

"Oh, I'm *great*." His voice was scarred by sarcasm. "I just got finished talking to Theo."

"Yeah?" Naomi's forehead prickled with sweat, and I cast a worried look between them. "Theo?"

"*Theo*," he repeated, fixing Naomi with a steely glare. When she didn't respond, he added, "You know, the editor of the paper."

Oh no. My whole body tensed as the color drained from Naomi's face.

"Oh, uh, right. Theo. Sorry. I mean, who can forget Theo? I never do because he's such a great editor, you know, always editing and stuff..."

I cringed as she babbled, and I stole a glance at Trevor who looked as horrified as me at the unraveling scene.

"Right. Except, Theo said no one is working on an article about the poetry contest, and he has no idea who *you* are."

Naomi froze like a statue. People noticed the conflict and slowed their pace to listen. Finally, Naomi spoke, but her voice was dry and brittle. "Webb, um, maybe we could go somewhere and talk?"

"Are you high?" His tone released the full flood of his anger. "I'll bet you and your friends got a good laugh from this, didn't you?"

"No!" she exclaimed and took a step toward him. "Please, it's not like that. I ju—"

"Sure," he interrupted. "Make fun of the guy who writes poetry, right? Well, I don't care what you or your stupid friends think, okay? I just wanted you to know your stupid joke didn't work."

I should have said something to stand up for Naomi, but I couldn't think of anything that would justify all the lying she'd done.

"Webb, please," she pleaded. "If you'd just let me explain, I—"

But he was already shaking his head. "Do me a favor and stay away from me." He turned and stalked in the opposite direction.

Everyone in the hallway stood silent as Naomi stared after him, her jaw hanging open in horrified shock. I reached out to touch her shoulder, but she pulled out of my reach. "Well, I'll bet *you're* happy," she hissed. "Go ahead, say it. You were right, and I was wrong." Tears sprung from her eyes.

"No, Naomi. I didn't want this. I swear." I reached out to her again, but she slapped my hand away.

"Leave me alone!" she screamed before she put her head down and pushed her way through the crowd.

I looked to Trevor, who nodded quickly and went after her.

"What?" I yelled at the hovering crowd. "Don't you have anything better to do?"

A few of them rolled their eyes and left, but most of them were happy to keep on staring until I let out a frustrated groan and pushed past a few people to dive into the ladies' room. I threw my entire body weight into the door and stumbled in, grateful to find it empty.

For the next few minutes, I stood over the sink and breathed. The pull of an anxiety attack tightened my chest. It took several minutes of deep breathing to steady myself. How had things gotten so screwed up? I'd told Naomi her stupid plan wasn't going to work. I *had* warned her. So, why did I feel so guilty?

When I closed my eyes, all I saw was Sonny's mournful expression pass through my mind. "No," I said aloud, pushing the invading image into the recesses of my mind. I needed to get out of there. I would text Dad, tell him I was sick, and go home. I splashed some water on my face and stared into the mirror, surprised by how gaunt and miserable I looked.

In the reflection, the bathroom door opened. I cringed when Sarah walked in. She looked surprised to see me, too. Maybe she'd missed the drama production we'd put on in the hall. She walked up to the mirror to check her hair and makeup, ignoring me.

I wiped my face and turned to go, grateful to whatever higher power was responsible for Sarah's silent treatment. However, when I got to the door, I heard her voice echo through the bathroom, "I'll bet you're pretty proud of yourself."

So close. "Not especially." I turned to her.

"Did you know Jesse and I have been together since freshman year? We met at a football game. I never missed a single game after that."

I crossed my arms, already exasperated by the conversation. "That's fascinating."

She shot me a dirty look and zipped up her makeup bag. "When his dad left, I went over to his house almost every day because he didn't want to leave his mom alone."

My stomach lurched. Sarah's sudden need to reminisce about her relationship with Jesse wasn't making it easy for me to keep him off my mind.

"It's not like I expected we'd be together forever, but I thought we'd at least go to prom, graduate together..." Her voice trailed off, and she looked at me. "I thought we'd at least have that."

Why was she telling me this? Didn't she know Jesse's attention was all an act? I opened my mouth, about to tell her how wrong she was, but she held up her hand and cut me off. "Then you come along, and he dumps me like I mean nothing. He gets kicked off the team, and it's like he's not even the same person anymore."

"I didn't ask for any of this," I argued.

"Well," she said, pushing past me on her way to the door, "whatever you say, *prom queen.*"

"It was all a joke." I blurted out.

She stopped at the door, her back still to me. "What?"

"I'm not going to prom, and I'm not going to be prom queen." My voice was starting to sound shrill. I hated talking to her about this. "Jesse and I aren't together, and we never will be."

"Wait a minute." She whirled to face me. "All anyone has been talking about is how you and your merry band of rejects are going to get you crowned queen." She studied my face, her lips pursed into a frown. "Why would you not go?"

I sighed and looked at the ceiling. "This is pointless." I tried to walk around her, but she moved to block my path. We were standing so close I could see the tiny flecks of gray in her piercing blue eyes. She looked more formidable than I'd given her credit for.

"Did he dump you?" she asked, her voice full of astonishment.

I couldn't look at her anymore. "We were never together."

"So, all of this—our breakup, his getting kicked off the team—was for nothing?"

Apparently, even Sarah was going to heave the weight of her problems onto my already burdened shoulders. Well, I had news for her: she was going to have to get in line. "Are we finished?"

She finally let me move past her, but on my way out the door, she firmly spoke to my back. "You really do ruin everything, don't you?"

CHAPTER 35

Frances

Mom came out of the bedroom with an armload of laundry when I opened the front door. She stopped in the hallway and looked at me. "You're home early."

My first instinct was to make a snide remark about stating the obvious, but the sarcastic retort fizzled as I walked into the kitchen and slumped into a chair. I felt defeated, and the task of fixing the mess I'd made seemed impossible. Mom joined me a few minutes later, sans laundry. The washing machine hummed in the background.

We hadn't really talked since my meltdown on the stairs. When I'd finished crying, Mom helped me to my room, leaving Dad shell-shocked at the bottom of the stairs. She'd pulled the covers back and tucked me in like she used to when I was a little kid, and I let her.

For the next few days, I laid in bed and read. Emma, Jane Eyre, and Mistress of Bleak House became my replacement friends. Any fantastical character that wasn't...well, me, would do. While I was busy hiding in my cocoon of literature, Mom occasionally poked her head in to ask if I needed anything. She brought me food and coffee, and she collected the plates when I was done. Not once did she ask for an apology for the things I'd said. For the first time in forever, she was exactly what I needed her to be. I didn't know how to handle that, either.

When I didn't say anything, Mom quietly made coffee and carried two steaming cups to the table. She placed one in front of me, and we both drank in silence. The quiet was a small relief, but the events of the day weighed me down so much that I slumped further into the chair. I couldn't keep the words in anymore. "I've screwed everything up."

She put down her mug and waited for me to tell the story. I started with the worst part and told her how I'd broken Sonny's tablet. I told her how I'd challenged Lena, and Trevor's plan to make me prom queen. She didn't seem overly surprised by the video of Jesse and Nick in the locker room, and I realized Dad must have told her some of it. She didn't interrupt when I explained Naomi's stupid plan to trick Webb, or Sonny's posters.

Her only visible reaction was when I described the things the football players had said in the hall. Her faced tightened, but she schooled her features and listened until I was finished.

Once I'd told her everything, she took my untouched mug to reheat it. There wasn't a hint of judgment in her expression as she placed the cup in front of me and sat back down, but it didn't stop me from feeling miserable. She took a long breath and said, "Franny, I owe you an apology."

"No, you don't," I said.

"Yes, I do." Her voice was tense. A sudden spark of emotion distorted her usual serene appearance. She ran a hand over her brow, and when she looked at me again, there was moisture in her eyes.

"I never wanted to hurt anyone." She ran one of her fingers over a scar on her forearm, tracing the white line across her wrist. It had always been there, but I'd never bothered to ask where it came from. "You know things were bad for me when I lived with Grandma and Grandpa."

I nodded, sensing that's what she wanted, but the truth was, I had no idea. Gramps and Grandma Baker were a goofy, loveable pair, always ready for a hug or dumb joke. It wasn't until Mom returned from rehab that the tension between her and her parents became more obvious. They still called occasionally to speak to me, but never to Mom.

"It's not an excuse, but you were right, I've just been fooling everyone."

"I wasn't," I said, shamed by the memory. "I was just angry."

"The truth is, I never completed my steps."

I stared at her, not understanding.

"I never finished step nine." She blinked rapidly as she fought another onslaught of tears. "I told myself you were fine, and I didn't need to make amends, but now I see that I just couldn't admit how much I'd taken from you." Her voice cracked, and the final barrier breeched as tears spilled over her cheeks.

I was horrified, even more so when fresh droplets hit my own hands. I quickly wiped my eyes, but I knew it was pointless. She'd already seen them.

She took a deep breath, but her voice shook with irrepressible emotion. "Making amends would mean acknowledging that I'd chosen alcohol over you." I could see pain reflected in her eyes, and I wondered if it was hers or my own.

"Franny, I am so sorry."

I wanted to say something to put her at ease. I wanted to tell her I forgave her or that everything would be okay, but I couldn't because I didn't know if either of those things were true. How do you tell someone you love that they've hurt you and would probably do it again?

"I know you resent the program, but I *need* you to at least try to understand why it's so important for me. It took me a long time to hit bottom, and I will be grateful to your dad for the rest of my life for taking me to rehab." She wiped her face again, but it was useless; her mascara had already made long streaks down her face. "You're wrong if you think your dad just took me back. He told me he'd stick by me only if I completed the program and went to AA. He said he wouldn't put you through any more pain and would file for divorce if I didn't get sober." She reached over and grabbed my hand firmly in hers. "Franny," she squeezed, "all I wanted to do was die."

I looked at her hand as it gripped mine and remembered the

months she'd spent in bed after rehab. When she came home, she was a sorry ghost of the electrifying woman she'd been.

"AA helped pull me out of that place in my head where I told myself I didn't deserve to be happy, that I wasn't worth saving. It's somewhere I never want to be again." She gave my hand another squeeze and waited until I met her eyes. "I think you know that place, too."

A jolt of sorrow seized my chest as the truth of her words rang in my head. I couldn't talk because I was afraid that if I opened my mouth, only sobs would come out. So, I clung to my mother's hand, desperate for something to steady me even though I didn't entirely trust that it would.

"I'm not asking you to forgive me," she said, "but I need you to understand that the program keeps me accountable, and the attention I give it doesn't mean it's more important than you."

It was too hard to say what I needed to. It was still too raw. Talking to her this way after spending so much time hating her felt strange, but something long-clenched inside of me slowly relaxed. "Okay, Mom."

She smiled a little, batting at her eyes with the back of her hand. "Okay."

CHAPTER 36

Frances

I got to school early, hoping to make it to my locker before Naomi and Trevor showed up. I figured the best thing I could do was give them some space.

Since Naomi and I always sat in the back of the science room, I wasn't sure how I was going to handle class with her. That dilemma was solved for me when I found Naomi already seated in a vacant seat up front, her back to me.

A little dejected, I dumped my bookbag into her old seat and hoped no one else would sit there. For most of class I tried to focus on our assignment, but Bianca, a girl who'd made a name for herself in the gossip trade, leaned over and whispered my name.

I ignored her.

Not so easily dissuaded, she hissed and tossed her pencil at me. "Psst. Fran."

I shot her an evil look. "What?"

Bianca was tall and slender and looked like she could catch a gig as a Brazilian super model. She knew everyone and wrote a gossip column for the school newspaper. In other words, she was not a person you wanted to tell your deepest secrets to.

"Is it true Naomi was stalking Webb Harris, and he had to get a restraining order against her?" She held a pen in one hand and a small notebook in the other, ready to jot down every word I said—and maybe a few I didn't.

"No." I turned my attention back to my book. "*But,*" I added, "I did hear David Slone has a crush on you."

Bianca's jaw dropped, and she practically climbed across the table to get at me. "Shut the front door!"

"It's true. He said he'd never seen anyone so beautiful in his life, but he's too shy to say anything. He's sure you already have a boyfriend."

She looked appalled. "But...but..." she sputtered, "I *don't.*"

That was not news. Bianca's last boyfriend dumped her for making his sister the subject of one of her columns. She was heartbroken, but not enough to print a retraction. Besides, she got her revenge when her next column was about how he'd thrown up all over himself on a roller coaster last summer.

"I tried to tell him," I said in a sad, wistful voice. "But he didn't believe it was possible that someone like you could be single."

Her face turned a shade of purple, ready to burst like a piece of ripe fruit. "Come on, Franny. Shoot me details. Is he hot? I don't think I've met him. What's he into?"

I looked at her, amused by her undivided attention. "Super hot, *and* I think he's a sophomore. That's all I know, but you better find him and ask him to prom before someone else does."

Bianca looked equal parts gleeful and panicked. It took effort to keep from laughing. The fact that David Slone didn't exist was beside the point. At least Bianca would be too busy searching for Mr. Slone to trash Naomi in her stupid column.

Bianca winked at me. "Thanks, Franny. I owe you one."

"Oh, no," I said with a sweet smile. "It's my pleasure."

The lunch bell rang, and Naomi grabbed her books and darted to the door before I'd even closed my book. I was *so* not looking forward to lunch, and I considered going to Dad's office to eat. But I was tired of hiding. I'd have to face everyone eventually.

I'm not sure what I expected when I walked through the cafeteria doors, but everything appeared normal. After getting my food, I headed to our usual table, knowing full well I wouldn't be welcome there. I didn't want to admit it, but part of me wanted to see Jesse. I wasn't disappointed.

As if he felt my eyes on him, Trevor turned around and spotted me first, and Naomi followed his gaze. She scowled and adjusted her chair so her back was to me again. Trevor placed a hand on her shoulder and cast me a warning look, not completely devoid of sympathy but stern enough to send a clear message: any attempt to sit there would be ill-advised.

Their angry looks struck me like foam darts compared to the razor cut of Jesse's eyes when they met mine. First, they registered surprise, quickly followed by a shadow of disgust before he turned away as if he hadn't seen me. Chris was the only one who waved, and I returned his acknowledgement with a half-smile. I knew I always liked that guy.

One person was absent from the table. I glanced around the room several times before I acknowledged the painful truth: Sonny wasn't there. I hadn't seen her since that day in the hallway, and I was too ashamed to ask any of them if they'd heard from her.

Disgraced and officially exiled, I headed to the back of the cafeteria to find an empty table. Unfortunately, the cafeteria was already filled, and there wasn't much to choose from. I spotted one lonely table, empty except for a single occupant. With a resigned sigh, I marched over and placed my tray on the table.

Nick looked startled when I pulled out a chair and plopped myself down across from him. His light blond hair was brushed down, but not so low that it covered the surprise in his eyes. He wore a pair of expensive looking jeans, and his button-down shirt was crisp without a hint of fading color. Whatever social glitches he'd been dealing with lately, they hadn't affected his acute sense of style.

"What are you doing?" he asked.

"Eating lunch." I pulled a book out of my bag, doing my best to ignore his incredulous stare.

"Yeah," he said. "But *why* are you doing it *here?*"

My first instinct was to tell him it was none of his business, but considering our long and sordid history, I supposed it was a reasonable question. "I'm not exactly welcome at my usual table," I said this with a casual air I hoped would stifle any additional questions. It didn't.

"Well, who said you were welcome here?" His tone was frosty, but a hint of a smile touched his lips. When I continued to ignore him, he tried bating me. "Trouble in paradise?"

I glared at him over the top of my book. Did he really have the nerve to enjoy this? "Could we not talk?"

"You're the one who interrupted my lunch," he said, suddenly looking bored. "I think I have a right to know why."

I tossed my book on the table since he obviously wasn't going to let me read it. "What about you? Where are all your devoted fans?"

He scowled. "I don't need those assholes," he said, unable to hide the bitter note in his voice.

His sudden mood change surprised me, but his admission that things with his friends weren't totally on board eased my tension a little. "Let's just say I've been banished," I said as a show of good faith.

"What'd you do?"

"It's a long story."

He leaned back in his chair. "You have somewhere else to be?"

I supposed Nick's recent fall from popularity did make him slightly more likeable, so I gave him the cliff notes of my recent transgressions. Surprisingly, he listened without making a single snarky comment. When I finished, his expression was stoic. "You really broke her tablet?"

I sighed. "It was an accident. Let's call it gross negligence."

Nick whistled and raised his eyes to the ceiling. "Hughes, I think you're screwed."

I rolled my eyes. "Thanks a lot."

Nick looked at me curiously. "You really think Harmon hung out with you just to get back on the team?"

I frowned and glanced over my shoulder at my old table. None of my friends looked at me, especially Jesse who seemed to be ultra-concentrated on his hamburger. "I thought he did, but now...I don't know."

Painfully aware that Jesse was not going to look in my direction, I turned back to Nick, who seemed like he had something to say but thought better of it.

"What?" I probed.

Nick shrugged. Whatever his thoughts, he wasn't willing to share them.

"What about you?" I asked. "You going to tell me why you've suddenly become a hermit?"

Nick glanced away. I gave him some time to answer. "No one took me seriously after the whole locker room thing." There was a softness to his expression that I'd never noticed before. "I thought those guys were my friends...but I think maybe they only hung out with me because..." he trailed off.

When he didn't finish, I added, "Because you were a bully?"

He scowled at me. "I was going to say popular." He sighed and ran a hand through his hair. It really was great hair, wavy and long on the top. No matter how it fell, it always looked perfectly styled. "I probably wasn't the greatest friend, anyway," he added, his voice pensive.

"Sorry," I said, simply because I didn't know what else to say. "If it makes you feel any better, I doubt I'd win any best friend awards either."

"Maybe, but word on the street is you're going to be prom queen." His tone gave away his surprise. "So, you got that going for you."

"I'm not going to prom." I slid lower in the seat. "After everything I've done, I don't deserve to be queen."

Nick didn't say anything, and his silence only made me feel worse.

After several long minutes, he cleared his throat. "Look, Hughes. There's something I need to tell you."

"What?" I asked miserably.

He stared down at the table, but shook his head. "Nothing, I mean, I'm sorry, okay?"

When I didn't answer, he added, "For the things I said in the locker room." Our eyes finally met, and I was astonished to find sincerity in his. "And for everything else. I've been a pretty big jerk to you."

I stared at him, too stunned to react. I touched the bottom of my chin to make sure it hadn't hit the top of the table.

Nick's face grew more tense the longer I was silent until finally he snapped, "Are you going to say something or just sit there looking like a coma patient?"

"Sorry," I said quickly, my words catching up with my thoughts. "I was surprised, that's all. You really surprised me." I bit my lip and added, "I'm sorry too."

He visibly relaxed, and we both went quiet again, digesting our newfound truce. "I'm not sure why we fight all the time anyway," he said.

I smirked, remembering the time in middle school when Trevor and I put a wad of gum on the top of Nick's deodorant while he was in gym. "Maybe because we like it," I mused.

He appeared to consider that theory with interest, and a slight smile spread over his features. "Maybe we do."

We talked about middle school for a while. "Do you remember what an anarchist Rick claimed to be? He's a unit leader in ROTC now."

Nick laughed and slapped his knee. "That guy is such a tool." He finished his last couple of bites of food. "You know, Webb Harris runs a poetry club that meets today after school. If you want to fix things with your friend, maybe you could talk to him."

I raised an eyebrow. "How do you know about the poetry club?"

"My younger sister is in it," he said between sandwich bites. "I wait around to drive her home."

Nick: former bully, super brother. I filed that information away for further examination. "It's an interesting idea, but what would I even say?"

He shrugged. "I don't know, but if you could convince him to take her to prom, she'd have to forgive you, right?"

I stared at him. "Nick, you're a genius."

He shrugged, seemingly unmoved by the compliment. "Yeah, I know."

The first warning bell rang, signaling the last five minutes of lunch. Had it really blown by so fast? "Thanks for your help, Nick." I grabbed my book.

He surprised me again by briefly touching my arm. "Hang on a sec." He motioned over to all my former friends. "So, you're still hung up on Captain America over there?"

I frowned. I knew who he meant but not how to respond.

Nick didn't wait for an answer. "I don't like him, but I don't think Harmon only hung out with you to get back on the team."

"What do you mean?" I asked, unable to hide my skepticism.

"Because," he said, "he nearly broke my windpipe just for talking about you. Plus, he's been giving me an evil eye the entire lunch period. I kept thinking any minute he was going to come over here and break my neck."

I had to employ extreme willpower not to turn around and look at Jesse, but I couldn't allow myself to spin this as anything positive. "He just hates both of us now."

"If you say so," Nick said with a shrug.

The cafeteria was clearing out, and I forced Nick's words out of my head before they could give me hope.

CHAPTER 37

Frances

The walls of the English department were littered with flyers for essay challenges and writing contests. I'd searched each room for the phantom poetry meeting Nick told me about, but I was beginning to wonder if the whole thing might be his stupid way of getting back at me. Just when I was ready to throw my arms up in defeat, I heard muffled voices coming from a room I had assumed was just a storage closet.

Before I could reach for the knob, the door opened and several students filed out. A smile touched my lips, noting that most of them were dressed in black and had long hair that was gelled to messy perfection. I was sure I'd found the right place.

When I didn't see Webb come out, I stepped inside and realized I hadn't been wrong about the size of the room. It was woefully small with no windows and only enough room for five chairs.

Webb was inside talking to a girl. She was tall and pretty with long, straight brown hair that fell down her back. She wore a black turtleneck with a fancy scarf even though it was boiling hot outside. It looked like her next stop was a spoken-word slam at the nearest Starbucks.

I had to clear my throat several times before they both finally acknowledged me.

"Can we help you?" asked the girl, not bothering to hide her irritation. I wondered if this was Nick's sister. She certainly had the attitude.

I forced a smile and ignored her. "Webb, can I talk to you?"

Webb did not look happy to see me, but he didn't tell me to get lost either. Instead, he said to the girl, "Aspen, can we continue this later?"

Aspen? I rolled my eyes at the posh sounding name. Webb also appeared to be doing his best English professor impression. I was about to forget the whole thing and tell Naomi she was better off without him, but the furious look on Aspen's face was enough to keep me motivated. I flashed her a smug look as she passed me on her way out of the room.

Webb gathered papers off the table and shoved them into a messenger bag, then looked at me. "Well? What do you want?"

I had no idea what to say. Apparently, I was no good at figuring things out as I went along. "Well, first...uh, hi, how are you?"

He sighed and rubbed his temple with the base of his palm. "Frances, right?"

I gritted my teeth but didn't correct him.

"You and your friends had your little joke, but it's time to let it go, okay?"

"That's why I'm here." I stepped further into the room. "To explain. No one was playing a joke on you."

"So, Naomi really does work for the paper?"

"Well, no," I said, conceding his point. "Naomi *did* lie about that, but it wasn't like a joke's-on-you kind of lie. It was more of a hey-I'm *totally*-into-you kind of lie." I cringed when I heard the way my words tangled as they spilled from my mouth. I sounded like a lunatic.

Webb's expression said he agreed with me. "I don't have time for this, and I don't have time for your jokes because I know what you people think about me." He tried to push past me. Luckily, blocking the entrance to this tiny room wasn't difficult. I jumped in front of him, nearly crushing us both in the doorframe.

"That's just it," I said. "You don't know."

He took a deep breath and let it out slowly. "I've known girls like

Naomi before, and I'm not interested in being a part of her stupid games."

I didn't know what he meant by "girls like Naomi," but his tone prickled my temper. "No, you *haven't*," I said. "Because no one is like Naomi. Who, by the way, for some reason thinks you're amazing."

Webb raised an eyebrow. "I have no idea what you're talking about."

"Naomi wanted to go to prom with you, but she was afraid you were too shy to ask her, so she came up with this crazy plan to trick you into taking her."

"*Trick* me?" If possible, he looked even more appalled than before, and I started to wonder if I was making things worse.

"Yeah, but in the best possible sense."

Webb shook his head as if he were trying to dislodge Naomi's crazy logic. "But I didn't even know Naomi before she asked to interview me. So, how could I have asked her to prom? And I'm *not* shy."

I gave him a pointed look.

"I'm *not*," he said, with more force.

"So, you mean to say that if you *had* known Naomi, you might have asked her?"

Webb frowned, and I could tell he was being careful about what he said. "How could I know that? The point is Naomi lied to me. If she wanted to go with me so badly, why didn't she just say so?"

I sighed. Of course he would ask that. "Because people do stupid things when they are protecting themselves and you want to strangle them but can't because you know the world would suck without them." I don't think either of us understood what I was saying.

"Look," he said, "I can tell you want to help your friend, and I guess I can appreciate that, but this is a little much for me. So, maybe tell Naomi the next time she wants to go out with someone, she should just try being honest." Webb squeezed through the doorway and started down the hall.

Thoroughly dismissed, I suppressed the urge to rage at his back about how lucky he'd be to go out with someone like Naomi. I had to face that there would be no shortcut to fixing things with my best friend. I was just going to have to apologize for the way I'd treated her and hope someday she'd forgive me.

However, there wasn't much time to wallow in my failure because as soon as I walked out of the room, a hand reached out and pulled me to the side.

My mouth opened to scream, but Naomi placed a finger over her mouth, telling me to be quiet, and hauled me down the hallway by the shirt.

She kept a firm hold as she dragged me into the nearest bathroom. I seemed to be spending a lot of time there lately. When the door closed, I braced for her anger, but instead, I was wrapped in the tightest bearhug I'd ever received, which I quickly returned with a sigh of relief.

When she pulled away, I immediately flew into the apology I should have given her the day before. "Naomi, I'm so sorry. I was just tryi—"

"I heard."

"What?" I asked, blinking.

"I came here to talk to Webb myself, but I heard your voice, so I waited outside and listened," she said with a sheepish smile.

"I was just trying to help," I explained, "but I think I made things worse. I'm sorry."

"It doesn't matter." She smiled, although it held a note of sadness. "I shouldn't have blamed you. It was my own fault." She looked at me seriously. "Did you mean those things you said? About how the world would suck without me?"

I took in her appearance. She wore a pink skirt over a pair of polka-dot leggings with a Queen t-shirt under a pink leather jacket. It was all so Naomi, I almost laughed out loud. "Of course, you're my best friend."

She punched my arm affectionately, but her smile faded. "I guess there is no point in talking to him now."

She sounded so down. I reached out and put my hand on her shoulder. "It's his loss."

Naomi forced another smile, but it never reached her eyes. "What about you? Are you going to try to fix things with Jesse?"

The mention of his name sent a spark through my neck and shoulders. I'd been working hard to put him out of my mind, but hearing his name reminded me of the ever-present pit of misery setting up shop in my stomach. It was pointless to deny it anymore. I missed him.

"I don't know," I said, failing once more to push all thoughts of him away. "I'm just so relieved you're talking to me."

She let the matter drop, but if I knew her at all, she'd be bringing it up again soon. "So," she said as we walked out of the bathroom, "I actually kind of enjoyed pretending to be a reporter, so I thought I might try out for the paper."

"Might not want to bring it up with Theo until he's had a chance to forget you were pretending to be a reporter."

Naomi grinned. "You see, Franny, it's all about how you spin it. You say I was pretending, but I say I have loads of experience with undercover reporting."

CHAPTER 38

Jesse

The day was off to a bad start. Mom had to be at work early, so unless I wanted to walk to school, I needed to get up. I burned my toast while watching TikTok, and it was too late to try again. Now, the math problem in front of me felt like something SpaceX couldn't work out even with the greatest minds available. Yet, I was expected to solve it *and* show my work in less than five minutes during a pop quiz.

Not to mention, I couldn't stop thinking about Frances and that asshole, Nick Temple. He sure didn't waste any time. And what about her? This is the guy who made fun of her in front of all his friends *and* got me kicked off the football team, and now they're best buds? I suspected Nick had a thing for her, but I never thought Frances would fall for that loner-outcast routine.

I groaned inwardly and dropped my pencil on the desk. The problem was *impossible*. I wondered if Mr. Pierce would give me a pass if I swore never to enter a field that required anything above basic addition.

"Harmon?"

For a second, I wondered if I'd said that last bit out loud.

The office aid, the same girl who'd summoned me to my meeting in Morel's office, stood next to Mr. Pierce and waved a slip of paper in the air. "They want to see you in the office," she announced with the doomed tone of a hangman. "*Again.*"

This was *not* good. I left my quiz unfinished on the desk. There was no point turning it in. I'd probably be better off taking the zero.

"Take your things," Mr. Pierce said. "They said you won't be coming back to class."

The girl was already out the door before I could ask what this was about, but I wasn't sure I wanted to know anyway. I did a mental recap of all the things I'd done over the last week. Aside from contemplating running Nick over with the driver's ed car, I was pretty sure I was in the clear.

The entrance wall of the main office was made of glass, and several office aides ran back and forth, delivering papers to different offices. A man stood in the entryway as I approached. He turned slightly, and I stopped walking.

At this angle, Dad couldn't see me standing frozen outside the door. Shock waves of panic raced through my extremities. How long had it been since I'd seen him? Seven months? Eight?

I took off in the opposite direction, but I only made it about halfway down the hall before he called out to me. "Jesse, stop!"

My pulse thumped in my ears, and my hands balled into fists as I skidded to a halt. I tried to steady myself, but my legs began to shake as I turned around.

He'd gained weight, and it showed in his face. His hair was longer too. He wore jeans and weird open-toe sandals like he was trying to look younger.

"I don't want to see you." My voice was severe. It was not a tone I'd ever used while talking to my dad, and it sounded awful.

I could tell by the tightness in his jaw that he didn't like it much either, but he didn't say so. Everything he said was always so carefully planned out. "Jesse," he held both hands in the air as if calming a wild animal, "I just want to talk."

"No," I said, my voice scarred with hostility. I turned my back on him and started to walk away. "You shouldn't have come here."

He followed me, his voice growing louder and more desperate with every step. "Jesse, I have to go out of town next week, and I wanted to see you before I left. You won't take my calls. You won't answer my emails. Do you have any idea what that does to me?"

He wasn't going to make me feel guilty, but I was afraid that if I looked him in the eyes, I would see something in them that would make me cave. "Does Mom know you're here?"

"You're my son," he said, his voice clipped. "I don't need her permission to see you."

The anger in his voice only reminded me that he's the one who'd blown all our lives apart.

I jerked my head around and found he was closer than I thought. His stern look told me he thought he was dealing with a difficult kid. He didn't *want* to understand how things were broken. "Leave me alone," I said stonily.

He reached out and grabbed my arm. His grip wasn't painful, but it was firm enough to provide my temper with all the fuel it needed. I let go of my backpack and threw all my bodyweight at him and he fell to the floor. His face was shocked, and I think we both realized how much stronger I'd become in our time apart.

"What did you think was going to happen?" I shouted. "You'd take me out for ice cream, and everything would be okay again? You *left us* for a new family."

"You're my family, Jesse." He didn't bother trying to get up, but his voice still held command despite his vulnerable position. "I'm still your father."

Rage seeped from my pores, but a trembling voice behind me sent all my brutal thoughts packing.

"Jesse," called Frances, and its effect was enough to cool the heated blood in my veins. I turned around to find her standing halfway down the hall, a look of dismay on her face. *What the hell was she doing there?*

Not wanting to think about how this looked, my eyes dropped to the floor. When I finally gathered enough nerve to look at her, there was a mixture of shock and something else in her eyes I hadn't seen before.

Suddenly, it was all too much. My anger, Dad's power grab, Mom's sadness, the team's resentment, and now Frances's pity? Why couldn't everyone just leave me alone? I snatched my backpack off the ground and stalked past her, our shoulders brushing on the way. "Go away, Frances."

CHAPTER 39

Frances

I'd been returning a book to the library for one of my teachers when I found Jesse towering over a man on the floor. Every nerve in my body triggered when Jesse brushed past me. I wanted to reach out and take his arm, to stop him and tell him how sorry I was but sensed this was not the moment for speeches. He looked so angry.

Before I could pull myself together, Jesse was already gone, and the man on the floor awkwardly stood up, brushing off his shirt and pants.

I didn't need to ask who he was. Even if I hadn't overheard their argument, I'd have known he was Jesse's father. They looked so much alike. He had the same sandy brown hair. If he hadn't looked so utterly miserable, I might have mistaken him for a much younger man.

He coughed, clearing his throat. "Are you one of Jesse's friends?"

Now probably wasn't a good time to explain why that was a complicated question. "Yeah," I said.

"I..." He hesitated. His voice sounded shaken. Whatever happened here, it hadn't gone according to plan. "Will you check on him?" He looked at me seriously, pain etched deeply into his features. "He won't talk to me."

The truth was, I didn't know if Jesse would ever talk to me again either, but the bell rang signaling the end of class, so I nodded quickly and ran in the direction Jesse had gone, hoping I could catch up to him before he got too far. When I turned the corner, I almost crashed into Nick for the second time in as many weeks.

"Hughes," said Nick, "I've been looking all over for you." His easy smile told me he was genuinely happy to see me, which was a welcome change from our usual passing scowls, but I couldn't help but glance over his shoulder to see if Jesse was anywhere in sight.

"What's up?" I asked hurriedly. A creeping anxiety prickled in the back of my mind. Even if I did find Jesse, would he even talk to me?

Nick hesitated, and when I finally gave him my full attention, there was something off about him. He looked unsure and a little... shy, maybe? Very un-Nick like.

"You okay?" I asked.

"Yeah," he said, "of course." His voice raised a scale or two, over-correcting his tone. "I got you something." He handed me a plastic bag about the size of a large book.

Unable to mask my surprise, I gingerly took the bag from him. The idea that Nick Temple would buy me a present, even with our new ceasefire, seemed ridiculous. My breath caught when I glanced in the bag and saw the Apple logo laser-drawn on a thin, sleek box.

My eyes shot up to Nick's, who smiled but quickly schooled his features. "It's not a big deal," he said. "My cousin works at the Apple store and owes me a favor." He paused, examining my face, and I glanced back down at the new tablet again, too dumbstruck to speak. "I figured you know someone who could use it."

I could almost feel myself melt into a puddle on the floor. How was it possible that Nick, of all the people in the world, would be there for me when I needed him?

I looked at him again, but it was like I was seeing him for the first time. "Nick, I don't know what to say..." I trailed off, failing to find the right words to express my gratitude. "This is the best present anyone has ever given me."

He looked away. "Like I said, no big deal," he repeated, and I tried not to notice how his cheeks reddened. "Listen, I, uh... There's something else I wanted to ask you."

There were a few students entering the hallway. Somehow classes had let out and I hadn't even noticed. "I was just wondering... if you'd worked things out with Harmon yet?"

I tried to ignore how my heart ached at the question. Whatever I'd thought he was going to ask, that wasn't it. "No...he's...not talking to me right now."

Go away, Frances, echoed Jesse's voice in my head, but somehow I doubted I could fulfill the request.

"Well, I was thinking...if he's too stupid to take you to prom, maybe we could go together."

I blinked at him. Nick just asked me to prom. I felt like I'd slipped into a parallel universe. What would I find when I got home? Mom passed out in front of the football game while Dad baked cookies for his next team meeting? Perhaps all my romance novels would be replaced with science fiction? I almost shuddered at the thought.

"You know," he continued, looking more vulnerable than I'd ever seen him, "after we spoke, I, uh...talked it out with some of my friends. I'm still up for prom king and everyone says you'll be queen... It could be cool, you know? If we both won." Nick's eyes were cast down, but then slowly raised his eyes to mine, shy but curious.

Why hadn't I ever noticed how incredible his eyes looked through the sleek, blond strands of hair that fell over his face. The whole thing would have sounded absurd a few weeks ago, but looking at him now, the idea of Nick and me standing together in front of the whole school as king and queen sounded more appealing than I was willing to admit. I shook my head, trying to dislodge the fantasy. "Nick," I said, "I'd love to, but I have this plan to fix things...and I think I need to go to prom alone."

He seemed to consider this. "Okay." He impressed me again by taking my refusal in stride. If Nick was upset about my answer, he wasn't going to make me feel bad about it, and I appreciated that.

We were both late for class, but I couldn't shake the feeling that I had to somehow pay Nick back for the brilliant gift he'd given me. "Hey, do you know Sarah Russell?"

He glanced at me skeptically. "She's a cheerleader, right?"

"Yeah. She's also Jesse's ex-girlfriend, and I think she might be looking for someone to take her to prom. If you ask her, she might say yes."

As soon as I'd said it, I was afraid I'd made the wrong move, but he seemed to consider the idea with interest. "I don't really know her," he said, "but...she *is* pretty cute. You think it would piss Harmon off if I took her?"

I could feel the corner of my mouth twitch. Apparently, the old Nick wasn't completely gone after all. "It might."

Nick smirked and slung his backpack over his shoulder. "Thanks for the tip."

CHAPTER 40

Frances

Sonny's house was in an older part of Deltona. Mature oak trees formed a shady dome over the path leading to the doorway, which was lined with potted plants in various stages of growth.

I hesitated before knocking. What if Sonny refused to talk to me? Or what if her grandmother ran me off? *I'd deserve it*, I thought. Regardless, I straightened my shoulders and clutched the Apple bag in my hand. Thanks to Nick, even if Sonny never spoke to me again, at least I could make this one thing right.

As it turned out, I didn't have to knock because the moment I lifted my fist to the door, it flung open.

"Frances, *mi buena chica!*" exclaimed Ms. Reina, who pulled me into a tight hug as enthusiastic as the first she'd given me.

"Hi, Ms. Reina." I winced at how guilty I sounded. Obviously, she didn't know what I'd done, or she wouldn't greet me so warmly.

I was quickly ushered inside and immediately overtaken by a pack of dogs that had me up against the wall in seconds. After my initial shock, I realized the dogs weren't as vicious as they were plentiful. There were six in all, mostly Chihuahuas and a couple of larger dogs who barreled over the little ones to get to me.

Ms. Reina yelled something in Spanish and most of the dogs backed off, but one big, shaggy mutt remained stubbornly by my side. I scratched him behind his ears, and he closed his eyes, leaning his massive head into my hand. The house was furnished in warm colors that looked like the desert, and family pictures covered nearly every available surface.

I peered at some of the photos on a long table in the entryway. There was a picture of a young couple holding a toddler with tight brown curls at a large rocky area that might have been the Grand Canyon. After closer inspection, I recognized Sonny's large eyes and marveled at how happy and unburdened they looked.

Sonny's grandmother stood behind me and looked fondly at the picture, although when I looked at her, there was pain seeping through her smile. "My son and his wife." Ms. Reina sighed wistfully. "Too young."

I knew it was rude to ask, but I couldn't help myself. "What happened to them?"

"Car accident. A year ago," she said.

My breath caught. I tried to imagine losing both my parents, moving, and changing schools all in one year, but I couldn't. I remembered Sonny's tears in the bathroom that day I'd found her. She'd cried for her mother, and it made me think about how I'd turned my own mom's offer to go camping down flat. "I'm sorry," was all I could manage without my voice cracking.

"I try my best, but...it is not like having mamá and papa, you know?"

I nodded and smiled down as the large dog at my side, perhaps sensing our somber mood, licked my hand.

Ms. Reina brushed at her eyes as she led me into the kitchen, all six dogs in tow, where she offered me a chair at the kitchen table. She immediately went to the stove and started dishing food onto a plate.

"I didn't mean to interrupt your dinner," I said, feeling like an intruder, but Ms. Reina waved off my apology and set a plate piled high with chicken, rice, and beans in front of me.

"Oh," I stammered, eyeing a serving of food big enough to feed a family of four. "I'm actually not that hungry."

Ms. Reina laughed and placed a fork in my hand. "Don't be silly," she said with so much confidence that I abandoned any further protest and tipped a forkful of chicken into my mouth. The food was incredible, and Ms. Reina was content to watch me eat for a few minutes before I asked if Sonny was home.

"Ah," she said, a knowing smile on her face. "Sonny does not live here anymore."

My heart dropped a little. "Where'd she go?"

"She is...*en capulla*." When it was clear I didn't understand, she added, "How you say, in her cocoon?"

I stared at her, and Ms. Reina inclined her head toward a door adjacent to the kitchen. When I'd first walked in, it had only looked like a closed garage door, but now it was slightly open, and I could just make out a pair of eyes staring out from the darkness. I blinked as the door slammed shut.

Ms. Reina shrugged. "Sonny has been gone two weeks," she said, looking solemn, but added, loud enough to be heard through the door, "I do hope she comes home soon."

I nodded, beginning to understand. "That's too bad." I raised my volume to match hers. "I wanted to apologize and tell her how much everyone wants her to come back to school."

"Oh?" replied Ms. Reina, casting me an encouraging look.

"Yeah." I thought hard about what I wanted to say, knowing it may be my only chance to get it right. "Sonny was a good friend to me, but I wasn't a very good friend to her." I paused again and took a deep breath. Why was it so much harder to say the truth out loud?

Ms. Reina smiled sympathetically and touched the top of my hand with hers, prompting me to continue.

"If Sonny comes back to school, I promise things will be different," I said.

No noise came from beyond the door, but just as I was about to give up, a soft click broke the silence in the kitchen, followed by a tiny creak of the door.

"Do you think she might still go to prom?" I asked.

"I hope so," replied Ms. Reina. "I always wanted a picture of her in a pretty dress."

"It's just, I have this plan...to make it up to her, but I need her to be there." I glanced at the door again. "So, if you see her, can you please tell her how much I need her help?"

Ms. Reina nodded. "I will."

I took a few more bites of food at Ms. Reina's insistence before standing and placing the iPad on the table. "To replace the one I broke."

Sonny's grandmother smiled. "*Dulce niña,* Frances. I hope she comes home soon so she can get her present." She gave me another tight hug before she walked me to the door. On my way out, I snuck one final glance at the door in the kitchen and smiled when I saw it was open just a little bit more.

CHAPTER 41

Frances

I was shoving clothes into my backpack when there was a knock at my bedroom door. Mom poked her head in with a hesitant smile. "Okay if I come in?"

"Sure," I said, my expression tight. Ever since our heavy kitchen talk, Mom and Dad had been checking in with me a lot. Although I found this new persistent attention a little annoying, I also had to admit, I didn't *completely* hate it.

"Why are you packing?" she asked, her voice tainted with an edge of alarm.

"I'm staying over at Naomi's, remember?"

"Oh," she chuckled, but it sounded a little strained. "That's right. You're getting ready for the prom over there?"

"That's the plan."

"So, we won't get to see you in your dress?" She sounded disappointed.

"Naomi's mom will take pictures," I said.

We were both quiet for a minute before she added, "And you're both going alone? What about that boy you told me about? Jesse?"

I zipped my bag. "There's no boy."

She looked like she wanted to say more, but maybe the edge in my tone made her think better of it.

"Naomi wants me over early," I said quickly to change the subject. This wasn't an excuse. She wanted to run through all possible hair choices and see which one looked best with my dress.

Normally I would never submit to this kind of torture, but it made Naomi happy, and I'd been trying to be a better friend.

"Before you go, can we talk a minute?" Mom sat on the bed and patted the place next to her.

I eyed the spot with trepidation. This had all the makings of another emotional exchange. A glance around the room told me there was only one convenient exit, but since Mom was closest to the door, my only other option for a quick escape would be to jump out the window. *Where was a rope ladder when a girl needed one?* I sighed and sat down.

She reached out and moved a piece of hair from my face. I forced myself not to flinch or wave her hand away, but my expression must have given away my annoyance because she frowned and lowered her hand. "You're so grown up. Pretty soon you'll be off to college."

I didn't know what she wanted me to say. I knew she wasn't trying to make me feel guilty, but I did a little.

"I just want you to know I see it."

"Okay," I said, unsure what she was getting at.

"What I mean is, I know you've had to grow up and be responsible before you should have." She smiled at me, but it didn't quite reach her eyes.

Why did these conversations always feel so sappy? Like those Hallmark movies Naomi liked to watch. Then again, maybe mothers and daughters were supposed to act this way, and we were the weird ones.

"Anyway," she continued, dabbing her cheeks with the back of her hand, "your father and I have been talking, and we'd like you to see someone."

I stared at her. "What do you mean? See who?"

"A therapist. Someone that can help you talk through the issues you are dealing with."

"No wa—"

"We've already made you an appointment."

"Seriously?" Did they think I was crazy? The idea of laying on some stranger's couch and telling them my problems sounded horrifying.

As if she could read my thoughts, she added, "It'll be a video call, so you don't even have to go to an office. You can have your appointment right here in your room."

I frowned. I still didn't like it.

"All we ask is that you give it a try." Her tone offered no hope of reversal. "There's something else. Dad doesn't necessarily agree, but I think if you have to act like an adult, you should be treated like one." She held out her hand and unfurled her fingers to reveal a set of car keys.

I looked at them, and then at her. "Those are your keys."

"Not anymore," she said. "Your dad and I are going car shopping this weekend. These are your car keys now."

I blinked. My *own* car. It was a freedom I hadn't dared let myself dream about. Suddenly I could see visions of me driving down the road, listening to audio books...alone. No one in the world to tell me where to go or with whom. It sounded amazing. Still, I eyed the keys with suspicion. "You're bribing me," I accused.

Her expression was serious. "Is it working?"

"A little." I plucked the keys from her hand.

She smiled and stood up, and I was grateful the conversation didn't get more intense. "I'll let you finish getting ready. Remember, I want those pictures."

It was an effort, but I made sure to hold my mother's gaze. "Thanks, Mom."

She smiled and looked a little lighter than when she came in. "You're welcome," she said and slipped out through the door.

Once I heard her footsteps hit the landing, I gripped the keys in my hand and danced a small victory jig around the room.

CHAPTER 42

Jesse

I slipped my arm into the suit jacket for about the hundredth time, checking to see if it looked right, but I was also sweating, so I took it off again. *I look like a dork.*

It was Mom's idea for me to wear a suit. I wanted to wear something more casual, but she insisted I would regret it if I didn't dress up. If I were going with Sarah, she'd probably have picked a tux for me. I pulled the jacket back on for the last time and walked out into the living room. Mom glanced at me from behind her laptop and squealed.

I rolled my eyes as she jumped up from her chair and immediately started to brush lint off my shoulders. "You look so handsome," she gushed. "What time is Chris coming over?"

"He called and said he was sick."

"That's too bad," said Mom. "How horrible to be sick on prom night."

I didn't say anything because I was super pissed at him. He hadn't sounded sick on the voicemail, and he didn't return any of my calls and texts. Now I was stuck going alone. I knew Trevor and Naomi would be there, but the idea of seeing Frances crowned queen made it the last place I wanted to be—and yet, I still didn't want to miss it.

"Well," Mom said, as she messed with my hair, "I have a surprise for you. I know you weren't thrilled about the idea of me driving you, so I got an Uber for you and any of your friends who need a ride home."

"Really?" I asked, excitement mingled with concern. "Isn't that expensive?"

"Don't worry," she assured me. "I've got it covered. Besides, it'll save me from having to haul my butt out late to pick you up."

I pulled her into a hug. "Thanks, Mom."

Her willingness to let me go on my own was a nice surprise. When I'd told her about Dad showing up at school, she'd immediately grabbed her phone and walked into the bedroom. I couldn't hear everything that was said, but the word lawyer had been thrown around a few times. It wasn't the verbal karate chop I'd been hoping for, but it was a start. Since then, Mom had been extra clingy, but I hadn't heard a thing from Dad.

"Love you, kid," she said, and squeezed me back. "Now remember, just because you don't have to drive doesn't mean it's okay to drink. I want you in the door before one AM, got it?"

"Got it," I said.

Her phone chimed, and she picked it up off the counter. "That's the Uber." She pointed a stern finger at me. "Be careful tonight. There's something else for you on your way out."

I walked to the door and grabbed my wallet and house keys. On the table in the entryway sat a small clear box. Inside was a pale-yellow corsage with small white flowers around it. I ran my fingers over the top of the plastic case. "Mom, you didn't have to do this." Why had she bothered? She knew I wasn't taking anyone.

"I didn't," she said, but caught my questioning look and smiled. "A nice man named Bill dropped it off for you. He said he thought you might need it."

I frowned at the box. Before I could dismiss the idea, I imagined how the corsage might look pinned to Frances's chest and cursed inwardly. *Damn you, Bill.*

"Make good choices!" called Mom from the kitchen.

"I will," I yelled back and grabbed the corsage on my way out the door.

CHAPTER 43

Frances

"I don't even know why I'm going," whined Naomi into the bathroom mirror. "I'll be the only loser there without a date."

"You are *not* a loser," I said, concentrating on not torching her scalp with the ancient hot iron she had in her bathroom. "But you will be the only person with a bald spot if you don't stop moving. Besides, Trevor and I don't have dates either," I reminded her as I unfurled the last curl. It fell with a light bounce in front of her face. "You look amazing."

Naomi grinned at me in the mirror. "I do, don't I?"

She wore a tight black dress with a high collar. It was dramatic and gothic, and it looked like it was made for Naomi.

I'd picked a simple yellow dress that let out at the waist and stopped right below my knees. It showed just enough cleavage to make me uncomfortable, but Naomi's ear-splitting insistence that this was *the dress* won out over my anxiety. My hair was pulled back in a bun with a gold headband to hold stray hairs in place. My makeup was simple, but it was there, which was a far cry from my usual look. The whole outfit had an unintended fifties feel. I couldn't admit it as freely as Naomi, but I didn't think I looked too shabby, either.

"So, what exactly did Trevor say again?" I asked.

"He said he was busy taking care of something and would meet us there."

"And he didn't say what he was doing?"

"I already told you he didn't," she replied. "Calm down; you're just nervous about tonight."

Even though she was right, I still opened my mouth to protest, but the doorbell rang and cut me off. "Are you sure Trevor said he wasn't coming here first?"

We nearly collided as we both rushed out of the bathroom at the same time. I managed to beat Naomi down the stairs, and after I took a second to smooth my hair out, I flung the door open, fully expecting to find Trevor standing on Naomi's doorstep. I was wrong.

Webb Harris met my shocked look with one of his own. Obviously, neither one of us had been expecting the other. I took in his odd appearance. Over a black suit, he wore a dark robe bearing the Slytherin crest. The outfit was polished off with a green and white scarf and magic wand.

"Who is it?" Naomi asked from the stairs, but when I stepped aside, she sucked in a breath. "What are you doing here?"

I quickly retreated into the living room, but not so far that I couldn't hear their conversation. No way was I going to miss this.

Webb's voice sounded nervous, and I tried to psychically pass my meager reserve of confidence his way. "I thought... I probably should have called first, but I didn't know... What I mean is...I wasn't sure I was going to come here until an hour ago."

Naomi's tone was cautious. "I thought you hated me."

"I was mad, but I think maybe I could have handled things better."

"Webb, I'm *so* sorry I lied to you." Her words came out in a rush as if she were afraid she'd miss the chance to say them. "I wanted to get to know you, and I thought it was a good way to—" she broke off, and I heard her strained laugh. "I don't always have the best ideas."

"Maybe," he agreed, but I could hear the smile in his voice. "You know, I liked hanging out with you, and when I thought the whole thing was a joke, it bothered me more than I was willing to admit." His voice lowered, and I leaned closer to the doorway, but still careful to stay out of sight.

"You liked hanging out with me?" she asked, her voice full of wonder.

I laced my hands together, willing myself to keep silent. Unfortunately, I missed the next bit of conversation, and by the time I caught up, they were talking about Harry Potter. I rolled my eyes.

"Just give me a second, and let me grab my robe and wand," she said in a rush. Before running upstairs, she darted into the living room and grabbed me by my forearms. We both silently bounced with joy, as much as we could manage in kitten heels.

"He wants to go to prom with me," she whispered. "He dressed up in his Slytherin cosplay because he thought I'd like it." She grinned, continuing to bounce as if she were on a trampoline.

"Of course he did." I breathed in her ecstatic energy. "You better get up there and grab your Harry Potter gear. You don't want to keep your *date* waiting."

"Okay, okay," she said with intense excitement, but before she darted from the room, she glanced back at me suspiciously. "How do you think he got my address?"

I shrugged and tried to keep my grin under wraps. "Google knows everything, remember?"

Naomi let out a tiny squeak of happiness before darting from the room, and I smiled at the sound of her quick footsteps on the stairs.

I peeked around the corner into the entryway.

Webb spotted me, and a shy smile curled his lips. "Frances."

"Webb," I said, unable to hide my amusement.

He cleared his throat. "You look...really nice."

I tried to ignore the note of surprise in his voice. "Thanks," I said, suddenly feeling self-conscious again.

"I should probably thank *you*." He gestured toward the stairs where Naomi disappeared. "For texting me this morning."

I shrugged. "Just thought I'd give you one last chance to make the right decision." It wasn't exactly like saying *I told you so*, but it was close.

"So..." he said, "I guess you're going to be prom queen, right? I mean, that's what everyone is saying."

I allowed a slow smile to spread over my features. "Oh, I'm counting on it."

CHAPTER 44

Sonny

I never used the lamp in my room because the larva preferred the soft glow of the Christmas lights strung across my ceiling. The converted garage had been fixed with its own bathroom and closet. Abuela did not want insects in the house and said they had to stay out here. So, I stayed with them. Tanks filled with caterpillars in various stages of growth lined the walls. When they freed themselves from their cocoons, I released them.

In the corner of the room, a coatrack sat in the corner with a white bedsheet flung over it. For background noise, the television played *Animal Planet* on low volume. I laid fresh milkweed in with a *Danaus gilippus* whose growth hadn't been what it should. I watched as his chubby form moved and contracted around the tiny white flowers without giving it a second glance.

There was a knock at the door, and Abuela came in. "*Prendí tu nuevo juguete, mi amor.*" She waved the new iPad in the air. At first, I didn't want the one Frances brought me. It wasn't the same as my old one and didn't have worn edges that made holding it feel like home. Yet, I couldn't help admire the clean and crisp new screen. A thin film of plastic on the front begged to be ripped off. I took it from her and set it on the desk.

She frowned. "You don't want to play with it?"

I shrugged, and she walked to the cocoon tank closest to the door. Bending over, she squinted and nearly pressed her nose to the glass. "It's funny how they build a home for themselves," she said.

I didn't think it was funny at all, but Abuela had a weird sense of humor. "They don't build it," I corrected. "They shed their skin, which turns into the chrysalis, and then their body dissolves inside."

"Really?" Abuela sounded surprised. "So, they use their parts to create someone new?"

"Not all of them survive," I said. "Some never come out, and the cocoon turns black."

"Oh," she sighed, sounding forlorn. "That is very sad." She glanced from me to the tank.

I walked over and bent down next to her. The cocoon was sea foam green with gold trim around the edges. I wondered how caterpillars knew the color of the ocean.

"I hope this one will come out," she said after a moment, then looked at me and smiled. "Or how else will it know how it feels to spread its wings in the sun?"

Without saying anything more, she ran a hand down my hair and walked out. I sighed and glanced at the sheet-covered stand in the corner.

After a while, the call of the tablet was too much to ignore. I took it from the desk. The screen came to life and its familiar glow made me draw a long sigh of relief. I logged in and linked it with my Apple account. Almost instantly, hundreds of junk emails filled my inbox, and I received a chat notification in the corner of the screen. I clicked the request and saw Dale's name.

Why aren't you in school? Are you sick?

Hellooo?

I had two weeks' worth of messages from Dale. Some of them asked when I was coming back, but most just described the things that had happened in class that day.

Rocky got in trouble for screaming in another class, and Mr. Hernandez had to go get him before they sent him home.

I flopped down on my bed and curled into the blanket, enjoying Dale's blunt account of events. At some point, Dale had invited Rocky and Gigi into the chat, and I had a good time scrolling through their messages, which often covered a full range of subjects from the new Batman movie to things that smell like Cheez-Its but weren't Cheez-Its.

Closer to the end of the memos, Dale typed:

Sonny, are you still going to prom?

I frowned and let the iPad fall on the bed. The room was quiet as I stared at the ceiling. Were there enough good cells in my body to help me dissolve into someone new? Is that even what I wanted?

The faintest sound of chomping cut through the silence, and I moved myself off the bed and gazed at the *Danaus gilippus*. His tiny jaws munched on the delicate milkweed, and I smiled.

CHAPTER 45

Frances

I hesitated under the balloon arch over the gym entrance and squeezed my eyes shut against the flashing lights. After I managed a deep, centering breath, I opened them to find a room filled with people I barely recognized. Everyone looked so adult in their fancy dresses and suits. It didn't feel like we were in school anymore. After this year, many of us would begin our lives, and I'd never see most of them again. A semester ago, it wouldn't have bothered me. So, why did my chest ache?

"Any open tables?" Naomi asked, touching my arm reassuringly.

I scanned the room and spotted Theo waving us down from a table near the front, so we all walked over.

"Here comes her majesty now," announced Theo with an exaggerated bow as we approached. Theo's date didn't look so happy to see us. Her pinched features were familiar.

"You guys just get here?" I asked, ignoring his date's pissy vibes.

"I've been here since an hour before the doors opened, covering the entrance. Which, by the way, shame on you for being fashionably late. Now I'll have to get a picture of you when you win. Stage lights are murder on the camera."

"*If* I win," I corrected.

My insistence that the crown wasn't already in my hands didn't faze Theo, but when his eyes fell on Webb, he paused. "Don't I know you?"

"Sort of." Webb glanced at Naomi who was shrinking back to

make herself small. "I came to see you the other day about the poetry article."

"Right, right. Sorry about all that. You ever catch the little minx that catfished you?"

"I did *not* catfish him!" insisted Naomi, outrage drawing her back to normal height. "I was being romantic."

Theo glanced between Naomi and Webb with interest. "Wait a sec. You pretended to do an article about this guy, and now you two are going to prom together?" Theo placed his thumb and forefinger over his chin. "Tell me more."

Theo's date rolled her eyes, and I realized how I knew her. She was one of Sarah's friends. Well, that explained why she looked so irritated with us.

Naomi gave Theo the low-down on her master plan. Of course, the spin she put on it made it sound much more idealistic than the restraining order situation it had almost been. Webb looked equal parts flattered and appalled by her version of the story.

"Desperate girl goes undercover in the pursuit of love..." Theo murmured to himself.

"Well, I wouldn't use the word *desperate*," said Naomi.

"Love?" Webb asked, looking a little pale.

"I like it," declared Theo. "Write it up and have it on my desk Monday morning. I have space to fill on page five, and it will make a catchy feature."

I shook my head. How was it possible that Naomi both succeeded in pulling off her stupid plan *and* landing herself a feature in the school paper?

Naomi beamed. "No problem, Theo... I mean, yes, sir!"

"Can we go, please?" complained Theo's date. "I need to take some photos with my friends before my hair gets all flat."

Theo slipped an arm around his date's waist and guided her onto the dance floor. "Keep it under fifteen-hundred words," he called as they made their way across the room.

Naomi turned to Webb. "It wouldn't bother you if I wrote an article about what happened, would it?"

Webb shrugged, the corners of his mouth curved in a subtle upturn. "No, but thank you for asking."

Webb slid a chair out for both Naomi and me, and I couldn't help but be amused at the gesture. "Thank you." I scanned the room. "Anyone see Trevor yet?" I was happy for Naomi of course, but wasn't interested in being a third wheel all night. Sadly, Trevor was nowhere in sight, and I realized he wasn't who I was really looking for, anyway.

Naomi turned to Webb. "Want to dance?"

Webb looked at her as if she'd asked if he wanted to be fed through a wood-chipper. "I don't really *dance*."

Naomi smiled and took his hand. "That's okay; I'll teach you!"

I cringed as Naomi nearly yanked Webb's arm out of its socket as she hauled him from his chair. "You okay here?" she asked, and I nodded, quickly tossing Webb a sympathetic look, but there was no way to help him as they were swallowed by a swarm of dancers.

After some people-watching, I decided to walk around. People waved as I went by, and I did my best to smile and seem happy, but it was a struggle. A few people congratulated me prematurely, and I gently reminded them it wasn't over yet. Others, like Lena and her friends, glared at me from the headquarters that was their table. Just one of the many reasons I would be glad when this whole prom thing was behind me.

"Fran!" a voice called. I turned and Bianca nearly crashed into me, dragging a lanky guy with glasses behind her.

"Hey, Bianca," I said, trying to cover my exasperation. "How's it going?"

She wore an elegant and revealing purple dress with her hair clad in perfect brown curls. A card titled "rumor notepad" was draped around her neck in a lanyard. Apparently, nothing was going to stop this gossip reporter from getting her story. "*A-maze-ing*," she said.

"We wanted to say thank you for being our own personal Cupid." Bianca beamed and slid an arm through her date's.

"I'm sorry," my gaze moved between them, "being your *what?*"

"This is David Slone," she said, practically singing his name. "Remember? You told me he wanted to ask me to prom? Well, I found him and asked him first!"

I blinked at David. He was so tall and thin, I had to look up to meet his eyes. He wore a pair of ill-fitting dress pants and a Dungeons & Dragons t-shirt. "*Oh*, right, David," I sputtered. "Wow, I mean, I'm so glad you two finally got together."

"You're an angel," she said, raising her voice to compete with the music. "Did you catch my column? I told everyone they were a fool if they didn't vote for you. Come on, David; I want to dance," she commanded, already swaying herself onto the dance floor.

David moved to follow her, but before he left, he leaned close to me. "I don't know who you are or why you told her to ask me out, but I owe you one." He winked and headed after Bianca. His moves were as smooth as a train of dynamite crashing into a chicken truck, but I smiled at his enthusiasm.

CHAPTER 46

Jesse

While scanning the gym for Frances, I almost ran right into Sarah. At first, I was too surprised to say anything, but cleared my throat and belted over the music. "Hey."

She didn't spit in my face, so that was a plus, but she didn't look happy to see me either. "Jesse," she acknowledged dryly.

"You look great," I offered, but wasn't sure she heard me until her pinched expression softened a little.

"Are you here with anyone?" she asked. Just like Sarah to skip the small talk.

I shook my head.

She frowned. "So, what? Better to come alone than go with me?"

I sighed and rubbed a hand along the back of my neck. "You know it wasn't like that." There was an awkward pause before I added, "You here with anyone?" I'm not sure why I asked, maybe I just wanted to know she didn't come alone.

"Yeah, I'm here with someone," she said. But she didn't say who, so I didn't ask.

"Look, Sarah. I'm sorry." I paused, not knowing how to finish. I wasn't sure I'd done anything wrong, but I knew I didn't want to leave things the way they were. "About everything."

She nodded, and although her eyes looked a little sad, her voice remained steady. "Me too," and she smiled. "Maybe I'll see you later."

As I watched her walk away a hand came down on my shoulder.

"Hey, Jesse!" Trevor exclaimed. "Good to see you. I wasn't sure you'd come."

I was surprised to see Chris standing alongside him. They both wore suits with a red flower in the front pocket. I almost didn't recognize Chris because I'd never seen him so dressed up. "I thought you were sick," I said, but my words hung in the air as my eyes fell on Chris's and Trevor's hands, clasped together.

Before I had a chance to process what I was seeing, Trevor smiled and slipped between us. "Wow, I'm thirsty," he announced. "I'm going to get us some punch."

Chris let go of Trevor's hand as he left but didn't look happy about it. We stood silent for a long moment.

"So, Trevor's your date?" I asked, the question coming off more like an accusation than I'd meant it to.

Chris tensed. "Yeah. That a problem for you?"

I was rubbed raw by his tone, but guilt cooled my outrage. I was the one getting this wrong. "What I mean is, I'm happy for you. I guess I just don't understand why you didn't tell me sooner."

When Chris didn't say anything, an unwelcome realization sent blood rushing to my face. Was it possible he had tried to tell me? Had I been too wrapped up in my own problems to notice? Frustrated, I ran a hand through my hair. The music made it hard to concentrate. "What about your parents?" I asked.

"I told them when Trevor picked me up," he said.

"How'd that go?"

His features softened a little. "Fine, I guess. I got the whole we-love-you-no matter-what speech, which was weird with Trevor standing there."

"I'm sorry if I haven't been a great friend lately."

Chris raised an eyebrow. "Jesse, it's not about you. I know I could have told you." He looked at me, a little color touching his cheeks. "I guess I was afraid things would change."

"Nothing is going to change," I said firmly and more of the tension drained from his features.

"So, you and Trevor. That's...pretty cool."

"I'm not sure I'm ready to talk guys yet," Chris said quickly.

"Yeah, okay," I agreed, relieved.

Fortunately, my phone vibrated in my pocket and interrupted our awkward silence. I answered the call with more enthusiasm than I had ever given an unknown caller. "Yeah?"

"Jesse Harmon?" asked a woman's voice.

I frowned and stuck my finger in my other ear to hear her over the music. "Yeah, who is this?"

"My name is Carol. I'm a nurse at Central Florida Regional Hospital in Sanford. I'm here with Mrs. Harmon. She's gone into labor, and no one has been able to reach her husband."

"She's in what?" My first thought was Mom, but it didn't take long for me to realize who she was talking about. My body tensed, but I didn't have time to be angry because the nurse kept talking.

"Mr. Harmon? Are you there? We tried everyone else on the list, but no one is answering. Can you come to the hospital?"

I couldn't process what she was saying. Labor? Dad? Go to the... "Wait, what do you mean go to the hospital?"

The nurse paused. "Should I tell Mrs. Harmon you can't make it?"

There was another beat of silence as Chris looked at me questioningly. The idea that Dad would put me down as an emergency contact was weird. What about Uncle Ray or one of his friends... There must be someone else Dad trusted more than me, right? "Tell her I'll be there soon."

I hung up the phone just as Trevor walked back, balancing three drinks. "Everything okay?" he asked, seeing my shocked expression.

"It's my dad." I downed the punch he handed me in one gulp. "I've got to get to the hospital, but I have no idea how. The Uber Mom got me won't be back until later." I was already sprinting for the door when Trevor caught up with me.

"Wait," he said. "What about Frances?"

I thought about the corsage still crammed in my suit pocket and how much I wanted to give it to her, but this was something I had to do. "Frances knows what she's doing."

Trevor sighed and pulled out his keys. "Here, take my car."

Gratefully, I picked the keys out of his hand. "Thank you, Trevor. You're a good friend."

"Yeah, yeah. Wipe that smile off your face, and be careful with my car," he called after me. "That's not the Batmobile you're driving!"

CHAPTER 47

Frances

I found Trevor and Chris near the entrance. They were standing close together, as if sharing a secret. "Hey," I said, my tone snappish. I'd been annoyed with Trevor since I'd heard he wasn't going to ride with us, and I didn't understand all the secrecy. "When did you get here?"

Trevor smiled, but it looked strained. "There's the beautiful prom queen now."

I wanted to resist the subject change but reminded myself that although Trevor was talking to me again, I was still on thin ice. "Hey, Chris," I said, softening my tone. "Did you guys see that Naomi and Webb are here together?"

"No," Trevor said, his smile genuine, "but I didn't have to. She's texted me fifty times since he picked her up."

I glanced around the room again and took a deep breath. So far, it looked like my big plan was going to be a bust, and I didn't know if there was anything I could do to fix it. But maybe there was one thing I could fix, if it wasn't already too late. "Have either of you seen Jesse?"

They looked at each other, and I raised an eyebrow. "What? He's not here?"

"He was," said Chris carefully, "but he left."

"He left? What do you mean he left?"

I must have looked upset because Trevor took both my shoulders in his hands. "Listen, don't worry about it. They're about to announce the king and queen, and I need you focused. You've got to go up there and finish this."

I shook out of his grip and took a step back. "You think I care about being queen? When did he leave? Did he say anything?"

"You just missed him," said Chris, but I was already out of the gym before he could explain.

I ran down the hall, the sound of my heels clicking on the linoleum. I crashed into the exterior doors so hard they swung out and banged on the concrete walls. The parking lot was nearly devoid of people, and several glances produced no sign of Jesse anywhere. I took a deep breath, equally crushed and angry that Jesse would come to prom but leave before speaking to me. I stood outside for a few miserable minutes, breathing and cooling my resentment.

Why the hell should he stay after the way I treated him? I turned and shuffled back through the doors. No matter how badly things turned out, Trevor was right. I had to finish what I started. But just before I made it to the gym, someone grabbed my arm. My eyes lit up with rage as I tried to pull away.

I recognized Greg right away. He was one of the football players who'd made fun of me in the hallway. His breath reeked of alcohol. I tried to shove against him, but he only tightened his grip.

"Coach's daughter," his words came out slow and deliberate as if he were having trouble getting them out.

I tried to wrench my arm free again, and this time it worked. He let go and stumbled back into a set of lockers.

I glared at him. "You're drunk. Why don't you have someone drive you home before you embarrass yourself?" I started to walk away, but he reached for me again.

He pushed me up against the lockers. "What's so special about you anyway?" He belched in my face, and I nearly gagged.

Anger flared inside me like an uncontrolled burn. Who the hell did this guy think he was talking to? I threw all my bodyweight into him, and he stumbled back. "I can't believe I let you get inside my head," I spat at him. "You don't decide my value."

He snorted and made a move toward me. Instinctually, I took a swing at him, and my fist connected with his jaw. Pain exploded in my hand. I doubled over, shielding my fingers.

For as much as it hurt, my punch barely impacted him, and he laughed. Of course he did. He laughed so hard he nearly fell over. "That's all you got? You punch like a prom queen."

My knee connected with his crotch. He sucked in a breath and fell forward, both hands moving to his privates. His wails of agony almost eclipsed my loud cursing as I tried to move the fingers on my right hand. Nevertheless, I stood over him. "If you ever put your hands on me again, you're going to be sorry."

"Ladies and gentlemen, the moment you've all been waiting for..." Kevin's voice boomed from the gym. "It's time to announce West Pine High's next prom King and Queen!" There was an uproar of cheers as I stepped over Greg, leaving him moaning and writhing in the fetal position.

CHAPTER 48

Frances

"Our new prom queen is..." Kevin paused as he slipped the gold-rimmed card from its envelope. Beads of sweat prickled my forehead. Beside me on stage, Lena's red sequined dress almost blinded me under the roasting stage lights. For the first time since I've known her, she looked nervous.

Nick, already crowned king, stood off to the side and waited along with everyone else, but all I could think about was my throbbing right hand. My battered knuckles threatened to start bleeding. I grimaced and hid my hand behind my back. Seriously, if anyone expected answers, they could ask the other guy.

Kevin cast me a bright, practiced smile, and I squeezed my eyes shut against a roll of nausea.

"Frances Hughes!" Kevin yelled, and the room erupted in applause. Before I could absorb what it all meant, Kevin placed a tacky glitter crown on my head.

Lena's shoulders slumped, and I *almost* felt bad for her as she shrank from the traditional congratulatory hug and stalked off stage.

Kevin shoved the microphone in my face. I recoiled as if he'd tried to hand me a live snake. He shook it at me again and silently mouthed, "Say something."

I took the microphone with my good hand and peered into the crowd. Naomi was right up front, her reassuring smile a beacon in the dark. The noise of the crowd died down in anticipation of whatever heartwarming platitudes I might offer as their newest prom queen, but I didn't have the heart to tell them that so far, the whole thing had sounded better on paper.

I was probably the most absurd prom queen of all time: a cynical, *dateless* bookworm who was sweating through her plus-size dress and sporting the busted knuckles of a prizefighter. So, how had it come to this? I looked into the crowd, contemplating all the twists and turns that set me upon the crooked throne of my high school social empire, and just knew that somehow this whole thing *had* to be Jesse Harmon's fault.

When words didn't come, Nick placed a hand on my shoulder. Even I couldn't deny that he made a handsome prom king: black tux, sharp features, and messy blond hair that was pushed down by a plastic crown. This small gesture of support revealed more feeling from him than I'd thought possible just a few weeks ago. But at the same time, nothing was like it was a few weeks ago.

"Wait," I said into the microphone. "I have something to say." The fact that everyone had already been waiting for me to say anything didn't seem to matter.

"I never wanted to be queen." This confession was met with confused murmurs from the crowd. "I thought if I won, I could prove anyone could be queen, but..." I trailed off and took a deep shuddering breath. "I was wrong. A real queen isn't afraid to be herself and is there when her friends need her."

Although it was dark, I felt everyone's eyes boring into me as I lifted the crown from my head. I smiled wearily at them. "Thank you, but this crown doesn't belong to me."

As if my words were a magical incantation, Sonny appeared in the doorway. She wore a bright red, studded tank top and rainbow tutu that frilled out all around her. On her feet were ballerina slippers laced up to the knee. Rainbow sweatbands adored both her wrists and her headphones hung around her neck. As always, her backpack was fixed securely on her shoulders. Her long hair was twisted into intricate curls that spilled over her shoulders.

It was an outfit worthy of a queen.

I called her name and everyone's gaze turned to the back of the room.

The crowd parted as she made her way to the stage. Nick stepped toward me, covering the mic with his hand. "Frances...what's going on?" When I didn't answer, he stepped aside.

As she got closer, I could see tension in Sonny's expression, but still, she climbed the steps with the resolve of a woman who knew where she belonged.

"Sonny," I said as we came face to face, "I think this belongs to you." I hesitated just before placing it on her head. I lowered the microphone and whispered, "You do want to be queen, right?"

Sonny turned to the crowd, as if considering the question for the first time. When she spoke, her voice held a determined edge. "Queen butterflies are always mistaken for monarchs because of their orange and black colors, but they are queens."

Kevin cut in, his face flushed so red that he looked like an angry tomato. "Frances, you can't just give the crown away," he insisted.

I'd almost forgotten about Kevin. I rolled my eyes as we both looked at him. "Why not?"

He shot me an appalled look but glanced at the restless crowd. "Because you can't. It's...it's...against the rules!" he sputtered as if those infallible words sealed his case.

I gave him a look that let him know where he could stuff his rules. "Watch me," I said, and I gently laid the crown on Sonny's head.

Once the crown was hers, Sonny turned to the mass of students. Before anyone had a chance to react to our sudden prom overthrow, she reached behind her and pulled a string from under her arm. In a fluttering wave, her backpack fell away, and a huge pair of butterfly wings unfurled behind her back. The cloth wings, colored in bright reds, blues and purples, stood to attention, held upright by a wire mesh. I recognized the floral curtains from Sonny's bag of junk, stitched in colorful patches. The wings lit the stage with tiny lights that glowed from inside the delicate material. The effect made the wings appear translucent and other-worldly.

The silence was overwhelming. Too shocked to respond, the audience stared at Sonny. My breath held as the seconds ticked by, and just when I thought my heart would explode from lack of oxygen, the crowd burst into booming applause, and I released all the air in my lungs.

I half expected Sonny to cover her ears or run off stage to escape the noise, but instead, she raised both her arms into a victorious V and yelled a battle cry of delight. Her call of triumph only seemed to ignite the crowd's enthusiasm, and the roaring went on and on, my own cheers and whoops lost in the chaos.

Delighted to no longer be the center of attention, I decided to make my escape via the side steps, but Nick caught up with me before I was halfway down. "Frances, wait!"

I turned to him, although I was more eager to get off stage and do something about my throbbing hand than have a chat.

"There's something I need to tell you." But whatever he said next was overpowered by the booming crowd.

"What?" I yelled.

"I'm the one who nominated you for prom queen!"

That I heard, but I wasn't sure I believed it. "You?" I stared at him, too many thoughts running through my head. *Where was a clue when a girl needed one?*

He gave me a sheepish smile, and it was harder than I'd like to admit to not close the distance between us. I decided I didn't need to know why; it was enough that he'd told me. "So, it's all your fault?"

"My...what?"

Before I could talk myself out of it, I drew him into a tight hug. "Thank you, Nick."

He hesitated, but returned my hug, holding on maybe a little longer than necessary. When we pulled apart, it looked like he wanted to keep his expression stoic, but even Nick couldn't hide the glow that spread over his face. I realized it was possible that I'd never really understood him at all.

He nodded and stepped back.

"Don't forget to give her a dance, okay?"

Nick glanced over at Sonny, now flapping her wings on stage for the uproarious crowd. "Sure, I can do that."

I smiled my thanks one last time. "I have to go." I ran off stage, shoving my way toward the exit with the furor of a heavy metal rocker in a mosh pit. I spotted Trevor and Chris still standing by the door. Trevor's smile was full of pride as I slammed into him, and he pinned me into a hug.

"I guess Jesse was right about you."

"Where is he?" I said, pulling away.

Trevor explained about the phone call and Jesse's flight to the hospital. When I realized he'd left not because he'd wanted to, but because he had to. I smiled. "I've got to go find him."

Trevor raised an eyebrow but didn't comment on how realistic he thought this plan was. "He took my car, so I can't help you there," he said apologetically.

"Forget it." I grinned as I fished my keys out of my dress pocket. "I have my own wheels."

"Well." Trevor beamed, pulling Chris closer to his side.

My eyes took in the two of them for the first time. I lifted my good hand to my mouth to cover my surprise. "Wait... Are you two...?"

Chris's cheeks turned pink, and Trevor nodded me out the door. "You better get going before your ride turns into a pumpkin."

I took the hint, smiled, and leaned in for another quick hug before I ran out the door. I stopped myself and poked my head back inside. "Keep an eye on Sonny for me, will you?"

"Go already, we got this," called Trevor.

I pulled my heels off and ran down the hall.

CHAPTER 49

Sonny

Aboy offered me his hand, and I stared at it, unsure at what it could mean until he asked me to dance.

The bright stage lights reflected off his crown. I only knew him as the boy who'd knocked my tray down. That was just a month ago, but now he was asking me to dance because he was king, and I was queen.

I ignored his hand and pinched a small amount of his suit jacket between my thumb and forefinger. I breathed a sigh of relief when he accepted this without question and led me down the steps to the dance floor.

The room quieted as a song started to play, and its gentle rhythm helped slow my pounding heart. The next bit was uncomfortable because neither one of us knew how to dance without touching each other, but he took the lead, holding a piece of each of my wings in his hands as we began to sway to the music. We spent the next twenty-seven steps this way. Eventually, I felt comfortable enough to lay my free hand on top of his arm. I decided to forgive him for the tray, since he was willing to dance my way.

"I'm Nick," he said, but my attention was all around the room. There were so many flashing lights that it was hard to stay focused. Naomi and her date waved from near the stage. She jumped up and down, and I was both happy to see her and grateful that she was far enough away not to invade my space.

Rocky and his girlfriend stood off to the side with Mr.

Hernandez. Rocky wore a mustard-colored jacket. His girlfriend was tall and wore a long white dress that narrowed at her ankles. She looked like a giant lily and Rocky, a bee.

Mr. Hernandez caught my eye, and he clasped both his hands in a fist and raised them in the air. Everything was blue and dreamy, like being under water. I felt like a dolphin gliding under the waves.

Someone tapped Nick's shoulder, and we stopped dancing.

Dale stood beside us. He was smaller than Nick and wore a Pokémon t-shirt beneath an oversized black suit jacket. His hair was slicked back, but I couldn't tell if it was gel or sweat. He was soaked, but I still thought he looked good. He stared at us until Nick asked, "You want to cut in?"

Dale nodded, and Nick turned to me. "Is that what you want?"

I nodded quickly and took my hand off Nick's arm without giving him a second glance.

Nick chuckled and raised both hands up. "Hey, no problem. Thanks for the dance, Sonny."

There was no awkwardness with Dale. He already knew what to do. He lifted his arms to chest height but didn't touch me. This allowed me to lay both my hands flat on top of his as we swayed to the rest of the song. We didn't speak because we didn't have to, and my first dance as prom queen was everything I hoped it would be.

CHAPTER 50

Jesse

The waiting room at Central Florida Regional was crowded and noisy. I sat next to a family whose kid had shoved a marble up her nose. Her parents didn't look happy, but the kid grinned at me, even as a big lump protruded from the side of her nostril.

I slumped further into my chair and waited for the nurse. It was weird that everyone kept calling Dad's girlfriend Mrs. Harmon even though they weren't married. At least...I didn't think they were. I tried calling Dad a few times, but like the nurse said, all his calls went straight to voicemail. I thought about texting Mom to let her know what was going on, but she would probably come up here, and I didn't think either of us were up for whatever that would look like.

Finally, a nurse came out and shuffled me toward the maternity ward in the main part of the hospital. I had no idea if I could be any help, but it didn't look like I was going to get a lot of time to think about it.

When I reached Kim's hospital room, she was sitting up in bed taking long, deep breaths. Her large, round belly filled the thin blanket that was draped over her. She looked at me, her features slack with confusion. "Who," she breathed, "are you?"

I stood in the doorway, unwilling to fully enter. "I'm Jesse," I replied. I tried to think of how to explain why I was there and wearing a tux, but I wasn't sure she cared about that part anyhow. "The hospital called me."

"Steve's son?" she looked appalled. "But why would they call you?" She took a few quick breaths that sounded desperate. Her blonde hair was plastered to her forehead with sweat. After another few moments of me standing awkwardly in the doorway, she yelled out in pain and grabbed the hospital bed rail. "Oh... Where is Steve?" Tears sprung from her eyes. "Why isn't he here?"

Maybe it was because the only woman I'd ever seen cry was my mother, but her tears were enough to chisel me out of the doorway. I walked inside and pulled a chair up next to the bed. "I don't think they could get a hold of anyone else. I'm sure he'll be here soon," I reassured her. "You want anything?"

She shook her head and bit down on her lip so hard, I thought she might break the skin. "I just...want Steve."

I nodded, because for the first time in a while, I wanted him, too.

Her body relaxed, and her breathing became less labored. "I'm sorry..." she exhaled, "...they called you down here. The baby is a little early and my parents are in North Carolina." She looked tired. "This wasn't how things were supposed to be."

Tell me about it. "You mean you're not doing this just to ruin my night?" I was trying to be funny, but she cast me an odd look.

She gripped the bed rail again and her body tensed as another contraction started.

"Aren't they supposed to give you drugs or something?" I asked, a little panicked.

"I wanted to do this without, I thought..." she yelled out again, fresh tears streaming down her face. "Oh, man... You must hate me," she cried, and I took her hand, which she grasped tightly.

"I don't hate you," I said. "Just breathe, okay?"

"We're going to," she breathed, "name the baby Joy."

I'd been pushing the idea of a baby away for so long that hearing her name was a shock to my system. I was going to have a sister, and her name was Joy. "That's a good name."

"You think so?" she asked, a ghost of a smile touching her face. "It was my aunt's name, but Steve doesn't like it."

"He's wrong," I assured her. "Joy is a great name."

She looked at me, and her eyes softened. "Your father misses you," she said, but before I could think about how to respond, her whole body tensed again, and she started her weird breathing.

I told her she was doing good, even though I had no idea if she was or not. The contraction ended, and she fell back in the bed.

We passed the next forty-five minutes this way. Occasionally, a nurse would come in, and I'd step out of the room. Each time this happened, the nurse would announce it wouldn't be much longer, but every minute that passed without my dad there, Kim's cries grew more frightened.

The nurse returned with some ice water, and I stepped out of the room so she could check whatever she was going to check. I connected my phone to the guest Wi-Fi and opened Facebook. Trevor was broadcasting the prom live. The video was dark, and it mostly showed people from the waist up. That didn't stop me from looking for Frances in the crowd. I imagined her dancing with a crown on her head and smiled despite the ache in my chest. She probably hadn't even noticed I wasn't there.

"Jesse!" Dad called as he ran down the hall. He looked awful. His hair shot out in three directions and his suit was wrinkled. I would have laughed if I weren't so grateful to see him. When he got to me, he leaned forward as if to hug me but seemed to think better of it.

"Where were you?" My voice held a note of accusation.

Dad groaned. "I dropped my phone down a flight of stairs. When I came home and Kim wasn't there, I headed straight here, but then I got stuck on I-4." His forehead prickled with sweat and exhaustion. "Did I miss it? Where's Kim?" he asked, his face full of fear.

"You didn't miss it." I directed him to her room. "She's waiting for you."

Dad looked at me seriously. "Jesse, you don't know what it means to me that you came down here. I hated how things went down the other day." He took a step back, surveying me, and frowned. "Oh no, you're missing your prom. Jesse, I'm sorry."

"See Kim first," I interrupted. "We can talk later."

He nodded and laid a hand on my shoulder before he dashed into the hospital room. His entrance was followed by the sound of Kim's relieved sobbing. I smiled faintly and retreated to the safety of the waiting room.

CHAPTER 51

Frances

The hospital's automatic doors swished open, and I barreled through, my heels discarded on the car floor. All I wanted was to find...

Jesse sat alone in the waiting room. I slid to a stop a few feet in front of him, not expecting he would be so easy to locate.

"Frances, what are you doing here?" he asked.

In a suit, he was handsome enough to make me temporarily speechless. Like a boyish James Bond, if there was such a thing.

"I heard you were here," was all I could manage.

He stood and we stared at each other for a long minute before he took pity on me. "You left prom?"

I took a deep breath, but my voice still shook. "I have something to say to you."

"Okay." He looked wary and vulnerable.

I knew that if I couldn't be honest with him now, it would be better if I just left him alone. "You were right."

Whatever he'd thought I was going to say, the shock on his face told me that wasn't it. "Right about what?"

"You once said that I try hard to make people think I don't care. You were right. It's hard for me to let people know how I feel because..." I bit my lip and searched for a way to make him understand something I didn't totally understand myself. "I just always assume people are going to hurt me, so I don't give them the chance to prove me wrong."

I hated how blank his expression was, but I didn't let it slow me down. "I know you weren't hanging out with me just to get back on the team. I didn't mean the things I said."

For a while, he didn't say anything. I considered that maybe it was all too much, too late after all. But finally, his stoic expression broke. "What happened?" he asked as he closed the distance between us. He lifted my hand in his to view my swollen knuckles.

The skin had begun to turn dark purple. My hand would be one giant bruise in the morning. "It's a long story." I suddenly felt exhausted.

"I've got time." He led me over to a chair.

I told him about the fight with Greg in the hallway.

"You should have called the cops," he said, his voice tight.

"He could still be lying there for all I know. I had to go in because they were announcing prom queen."

We didn't say anything for a while, but I was content to just sit there with him, especially since he hadn't let go of my hand.

"So," he started, his voice more casual, "am I looking at the bruised knuckles of our new prom queen?"

I laughed. Even though it had been less than an hour since the crowning ceremony, prom already felt like ages ago. "Well," I said, "for about five minutes." I filled him in on the rest of the night and enjoyed the awe on his face.

"I can't believe you gave it up just like that... You worked so hard."

"Not really. Trevor and Sonny did most of the work. I wish you could have seen her. She looked perfect with that crown and her wings," I recalled wistfully.

"Hey." He pulled out his phone. "Trevor was streaming the prom earlier. Maybe we can still watch some of it."

We huddled around his phone. Sure enough, Trevor's live stream was still going, and why not? It was Trevor, after all. Prom was roaring, and we caught some glimpses of people we knew.

"Oh look!" I said. "There's Nick."

"Is that Sarah with him?" asked Jesse.

I grinned a little, casting him some side eye. With satisfaction, I noted that Sarah wore the pink dress after all.

The rhythm of the music changed, and a long conga line formed with Sonny at the head. The person behind her held on to her wings instead of her shoulders. I shook my head but couldn't keep my happiness from swelling faster than my bruised knuckles. "She's already a better prom queen. I never would have been that much fun."

"Oh, hey!" Jesse said suddenly and reached into his pocket. "I have something for you."

I watched as he pulled a plastic box from the large pocket on the front of his suit jacket. The small container had been severely dented by its mode of travel, but contained a perfect yellow corsage. My mouth formed a silent "o" as I watched him gently pull the flower from the box.

"Where did you get that?" I asked breathlessly, but he didn't answer. He was too busy trying to pin it on my dress. He almost stuck me a few times in what I could only assume was a controlled effort to not accidentally touch my boob. He eventually managed it, and I breathed a satisfied sigh. It matched my dress perfectly.

"Thank you," I said, dazzled once again.

"You know," he glanced around the empty waiting room, "we could dance if you wanted." Without waiting for an answer, Jesse held his hand out. "Care to, Your Majesty?"

I laughed and took his outstretched hand. "Dance to what?"

"I could play something on my phone." He placed the phone on one of the chairs and soft instrumental music poured from the tiny speaker.

He took my good hand in his and led me into a slow dance. His steps were so natural that I would have thought he taught lessons on the side. Suddenly, Jesse spun me into a twirl and came close to bouncing me off one of the chairs before he tugged on my arm and pulled me back like a yo-yo.

"Hey," I protested as he took my hand in his again. "You've got to warn a girl before you make a move like that."

He grinned at me. "What's the fun in that?"

I made an unladylike sound in response and snaked my arms around his waist. My head rested on his shoulder, and I became lost in the hypnotic swaying.

After a while, Jesse nudged me. "You didn't fall asleep on me, did you?"

"Nope." I smiled into his shoulder. "Just happy."

"Oh?" He pulled away to look at me. "Does that mean you like me?"

I shrugged indifferently, but he wasn't giving up so easily.

"Admit it," he said. "You like me, don't you, Frances?"

I rolled my eyes, and as punishment he dipped me dramatically. I almost screamed, convinced I was too heavy to hold despite his firm grip on my back. "Hey!"

"I'm not letting you back up until you say it."

"I hope you have strong arms."

He grinned. "I could do this all night."

My jaw set. If anyone else came into the waiting room, they would find us frozen in this position, but I was delighted to find that I didn't care.

"I see a woman may be made a fool, if she had not a spirit to resist," he said casually.

I blinked at him. "Did you just quote Shakespeare?"

"Say it, Frances."

My mouth opened to protest, but before I got the words out, Jesse pulled me up until my lips met his. It was a long, slow kiss that left me feeling dizzy.

When we finally broke apart, I smiled. "I hate you, Jesse Harmon."

About the Author

Robin Mimna's first book *Hating Jesse Harmon* won the 2019 Young Adult Gold Metal and Best Unpublished Book of the Year at the Florida Writers Association's Royal Palm Awards. Her work has been published in Calliope Magazine and Deep South Magazine. Robin lives in the historic city of Lake Helen, Florida with her dog Harley and two lazy cats. She's an enthusiastic history nerd and blogger. When she's not writing she works as a service coordinator and is finishing her degree in creative writing at the University of Central Florida. She has served as a board member for the Autism Society of Greater Orlando, volunteers for the Enterprise Museum and currently serves on the board for the West Volusia Historical Society, the Lake Helen League for Better Living and Lake Helen Pride. If you want to know more about Robin's work, please visit her website at http://www.robinmimna.com, where you can sign up to receive information about upcoming releases.

This has been an
Immortal Production

CPSIA information can be obtained
at www.ICGtesting.com
Printed in the USA
LVHW042026011122
732103LV00003B/318

9 781953 491404